RELATIVE DECEIT

JANUARY KELLY

www.januarykelly.com

Follow on Facebook:

https://www.facebook.com/profile.php?id=100067850730415

Instagram:

https://www.instagram.com/januarykelly.author/?next=%2F

Also By

Paranormal Romantic Suspense
The Hidden Series:
The Night They Knew- a short story from The Hidden
Hidden Intent
Smoke and Shadow
Relative Deceit
Standalone:
The Last Lament of the Late Shawn Reilly
Contemporary Fiction
All These Days

For Lilith...

My sister from another mister and the gauge by which all good humans are measured.

Walking with a friend in the dark is better than walking alone in the light. —Helen Keller

Prologue

Max sat the phone receiver back on its cradle. Turning down the volume on the small portable television, he watched a long, black car pull just outside the gate. A man stepped out and stood just outside the door of the glossy vehicle, arms crossed behind his back.

The handsome man's pale skin and white blonde hair seemed to glow like a halo under the moonlight as he waited just beyond the gate of chain link and razor wire. Max, dressed in his tight-fitting tan uniform, sat in the tiny steel box that served as a guard shack, eyeing the Pale Man suspiciously. He noticed the Pale Man was dressed in an expensive navy suit and silk tie which only added to his seemingly no-nonsense, all-business presence.

In the near distance, the lone guard heard the clanking of locks and buzzers getting progressively closer to him. It wouldn't be long now. Max eyed his half-eaten sandwich and wanted a bite. He wished all of this could have waited until after his dinner break.

Soon, a medium-built, older man with dark hair emerged from the heavy security door flanked by another officer sporting the same ill-fitting attire as Max. The Old Man shuffled closer to the gate. An alarm sounded harshly through the night air as Max pushed a button to a metal barrier and the world swung open to him.

"Good evening, my son," the Pale Man greeted him with a wide smile.

Max noticed his perfect white teeth seemed to almost glow like his hair in the cast of the moon.

Relief washed over the dark-headed man's worn face as he fell to one knee, "My savior."

"Shhh...come now. You are no feeble, ordinary man. You are the sword...the bringer of justice. Do not bury your head in reverence any longer. You will sit at His right hand," The Pale Man replied as he touched the Old Man's elbow, instructing him to rise.

The Old Man swallowed hard as he met the Pale Man's eyes. Even in the light of a full moon, he noticed they were a darker shade than when he first visited. Possibly a trick of the light. It didn't matter as this man was a true messenger and served Him. *He* wanted to serve Him. When the Pale Man proposed the deal of a lifetime, he thought it was too good to be true. He didn't believe him and demanded the Pale Man prove it. He told the Pale Man if he could fulfill his promise, he would swear his life as allegiance. And now here the Pale Man stood, draped in cosmic glory making good on his end of the bargain.

Now it was time to fulfill his destiny.

He bowed his head only slightly, "I live to serve Him."

"Good," The Pale Man purred. "Come. The car is waiting and I'm sure you're hungry. I'll take you to where you will do your good work."

He looked just beyond where the Pale Man motioned to see a black limousine waiting. He felt wildly underdressed and a little embarrassed with his appearance as he gazed at the sleekness of the car. His tattered shirt and jeans were a size too large and his cheap tennis shoes made squeaking sounds as he walked over the rough pavement. The

Pale Man's smile never faded as he slid onto the dark leather seat next to him.

As if he could read the Old Man's thoughts, The Pale Man patted his arm, "Don't worry about your attire. We'll find you something a little more...suitable."

The door snapped shut with a soft *click*. The car wasted no time speeding away as Max turned the sound up on his television and finished his dinner.

1

Sunlight filtered through the half-moon-shaped stained glass window with beams of blue, red, and yellow dancing on the soft-down comforter. The sweet, early morning summer breeze filtered through the open window just over the head of the bed, making the thin curtains billow lightly. Derek stretched his arms wide and pulled a sleeping Siobhan closer. She rolled into his hold and wrapped her bare leg over his underneath their warm covers. She ran her hand over his hip and along his ribcage until it peeked out of the blanket allowing her pale blue, brilliant-cut engagement ring to glitter in the colorful light.

"You know that tickles," Derek smiled, his eyes still closed.

Siobhan stretched the sleep out of her muscles, "Sorry about that...what time did you get in?"

"Around two," he yawned.

Siobhan opened her eyes a little wider to inspect him. She quickly assessed every exposed area of flesh for new battle wounds but found none. Derek was the Hidden's guardian for the city of Portland and it was normal for him to be called away at all hours to deal with some kind of supernatural clash. Most of the recent issues had more to do with making sure the Changeling-Fae war didn't spill out of the Hidden and into the Known than anything else. The week prior,

Derek spent more time raiding potential Changeling hideouts in the area with his fellow Forehelien soldiers than he did working his *actual* job at his tattoo studio.

Derek wove his fingers with Siobhan's, twirling the ring on her hand. Leaning over, he brushed the strands of auburn from her cheek and kissed her. She felt his breath on her face as he exhaled and pulled away. The pair snuggled back in together, wrapping themselves around each other tightly. Siobhan pulled her leg along his again, feeling his muscles with her foot. She drew the covers over her head, put her lips on his left hip, and kissed it lightly.

Derek moaned softly.

Siobhan's tongue ran a trail from his solar plexus to his clavicle, as her breasts pressed tight against his chest. She kissed him behind his ear, biting his lobe gently. The scent from his skin still smelling fresh from his middle of the night shower; like ocean water and moss. She breathed him in and her heart skipped. Derek smiled, groaning in delight before grabbing her around the arms, and rolling her on the bed as he climbed on top of her, pinning her arms above her head.

"I thought we weren't doing this until after the wedding?" he smirked down at her. "That's what *you* said, right?"

Siobhan pursed her lips, "I don't think I can wait that long."

He kissed her neck, slowly running his hands along her body, "It's only two more days."

"It's already been two days since we made this deal...it's not fair," she laughed playfully.

Derek stopped, locking eyes with her.

"*We?* There was no *we* in that agreement kent," Derek guffawed, continuing to run a trail of soft kisses along her neck and shoulder.

Her eyes widened as he pressed against her, "Feels like you clearly think it's a trash arrangement, too."

Derek groaned again, "No...*we* promised...no sex before our honeymoon."

He watched her start pouting but knew she was faking and curled closer to her.

"Can you believe in two days we'll be Mr and Mrs Argent?" Derek purred in her ear.

Siobhan rolled closer, kissing his cheek, "Who says I'm taking your name?"

She did her best to hide her devious grin on his shoulder.

"What? I thought you wanted..." he stuttered nervously until he felt her shoulders shudder in repressed giggles.

"Damn it! I can't believe I fell for that...again," he burst into laughter, rolling over on her, and resumed tickling her. Siobhan roared with laughter as their nude bodies twisted in and out of the blankets as they wrestled. A sudden high-pitched cry down the hallway stopped them cold. Zeus, their eighty-pound Doberman-Rottweiler mix, who had been snoring comfortably, lifted his head at full attention at the sharp sound. Standing from his bed on the floor, he padded his way to the door and sniffed.

"Shhhh...maybe she'll go back to sleep," Derek whispered.

"Not likely...I think that's her *I'm hungry* cry. Pretty sure it's Theo's turn anyway," Siobhan giggled softly.

"It still cracks me up...Theo... a father," Derek chuckled.

"Hey...he's a great dad," she said in her friend's defense.

He propped himself up on his elbow, "No...no, he *is* a great dad... I just find it amusing that the same guy that used to chase skirts in literally every bar in Portland is now an overprotective super dad...of a *daughter* no less...I'm proud of him."

"I'm proud of you," she smiled back. "There aren't a lot of people that would take on another family."

"Another family? They *are* my family...and this house...this house is made to have a family in it. I promised my mom and Megan that I would keep them safe...there's no better place than here," he explained.

Siobhan sighed contently, "You're right... And a member of this family is hungry and if her dad doesn't get my precious goddaughter her bottle..."

Her voice trailed off as the crying finally became distant and soft.

Zeus whined, looking from the door to the couple. Derek threw off the few blankets that still covered him to open it, releasing the canine. He made his way back to the bed and flopped down beside Siobhan.

"So, tonight... the last of the pre-wedding festivities for Arvendon, the Komma...Mom said we need to be there at seven," he kissed her face and down her neck.

"Haven't there been enough parties for us?" she giggled. "I mean, the engagement party, the bridal brunch, formal dinner with the Order, and now this...it's kinda a lot. And we haven't even gotten married."

"I know...apparently it's all tradition. Tonight is more like a dual bachelor, bachelorette party. I hear they can get pretty wild," he continued to make his way down her clavicle and shoulder with gentle kisses.

"Wait...who's invited to this thing?" she leaned away from his affections.

Derek laughed, "Close friends, I think. Megan's sister is even coming over to babysit for the night."

Siobhan became quiet for a long moment.

"Reek...I love you. And...I'm so excited to spend the rest of my life with you, but..." she sighed.

"What is it?" he sat up again, this time concern furrowed in his brow.

She shook her head, "I don't know…Don't get me wrong, I'm so grateful for everything your mom, Tara…hell, even Casius has done. But…I just kind of wish we could just have something small, intimate, you know."

Derek paused and his eyes gazed over her face.

"I'm sorry, Von. I never thought about how much this would bother you. I just got so wrapped up in what the damn tradition dictates…I never thought about how anxious all this would make you," he apologized.

"I'm not anxious," she leaned her head back in the sun that poured from the window over their bed, "I'm just…Look, I know this is just part of our lives now…just takes some getting used to, you know? All the attention and…pageantry."

"I get it… Sometimes I feel like with all the damn *ascension* talk, everything is running away with us." Narrowing his dark eyes, he concentrated on her face, "You're not having second thoughts are you?"

A bright smile spread across her lips as she raised up to kiss him.

"About marrying you? Not even a little bit."

Derek smiled, slowly kissing her back, "Good. Now, how about we have some fun and watch the new dad burp our goddaughter."

After a quick dressing, the couple made their way down the wooden staircase, into the large, airy kitchen. It had taken Siobhan and Megan the better part of a year, but they were able to do something that no one had ever done before: they taught Theo how to make coffee. And it turned out that with a lot of practice, it was something he became quite good at doing.

This morning, its alluring smell met the couple as they found Theo feeding his four-month old daughter, Nerissa, in the cradle of his arm. Siobhan started to giggle the second she laid eyes on him, and poked an elbow into Derek's side. He nearly bit his own lip in half to keep from laughing out loud and startling the drowsy baby. The pair couldn't help but stare in amusement at Theo's choice of attire. He swayed easily as he cradled the baby in the crook of his arm holding the bottle upright, the thick tan pants with reflective tape and heavy looking shirt making a soft *swish swish swish* as he moved.

Derek poured himself a cup of coffee from the glass French press, "Nice pants man."

"Is that a new shirt?" Siobhan commented as she reached to check the tag next to Theo's neck.

"Hey...when you two raise a child that essentially has dragon DNA, then you can judge the clothing," he stated emphatically. "And, to answer your question, it *is* a new shirt...its flame retardant," he muttered.

Derek and Siobhan couldn't help themselves and rolled with laughter as Megan made her way sleepily into the room with them.

"Good morning," she yawned. "What's so funny?"

Derek poured her a cup of coffee, then offered her the cream, "Drink the coffee...then look at the man you decided to have a child with."

Turning around slowly, Megan took in the scene. As the information was finally processed, she rolled her eyes dramatically, "Oh my God. What the hell are you wearing? Let me guess...it's flame retardant. And where did you get the firemen's pants? Theodore Stephen, I'm taking away your credit cards."

"But... I...she...." he stammered as he looked from his girlfriend to his grinning daughter.

"They're just little flames...and it only happens when she burps," Megan reached into his arms, picking Nerissa up. "Huh, baby girl? And she'll learn how to control it...she's just little," she cooed at their daughter as the drowsy baby giggled.

Theo looked incredulously at the group as they laughed.

"Oh, come on guys...not fair," he muttered.

Zeus, who had been following whoever was holding Nerissa, padded over to Theo and placed his enormous square head in the man's hand.

Theo scratched the dog's ears, "You get it? Right boy?"

Zeus whined.

Siobhan patted his arm as she hugged her warm cup close to her chin, "We're only teasing, *Theodore*... but you really got to lose the pants."

2

With the large wedding ceremony just days away, it was all hands on deck for Derek, Siobhan, and their friends. The couple packed their bags and, using the doorway in the kitchen, made their way into Julia's office at Arvendon. While the final pre-wedding party would take place at their favorite watering hole in Portland, James Station, the remainder of the hours would be spent putting the finishing touches on the ceremony and reception that would take place in the Hidden. It wasn't only a joyous occasion for her Sovereign because she would be gaining a daughter, whom she already loved as her own, but also one of great jubilation for the entirety of the supernatural world as Derek would be assumed as the next in line to rule after his mother. The House of Silver Light, the ruling house of Witches in the Hidden and the house where Julia and Derek descended, was excited for the event as the past several months had brought with it a seemingly unending onslaught of arbitration among the other member houses of the Order.

The original matter at hand presented before the council regarded Derek's divided loyalty. Was he truly prepared to defend and counsel the Order and by extension, the residents of the Hidden in matters of state when he himself had, only just a few years prior, come into the fold? How would his coupling with an ordinary human affect his ability to rule in the future for the betterment of the Hidden and its residents? Would he be able to separate his affections for the human world and keep knowledge of the Hidden secret if required for impartiality? But the most sensitive of these was the question of whether Derek's own magical power was developed enough to even hold the title of Sovereign Witch. Eventually, and just two days ago, the Order conceded on all points that Derek Argent of Portland Known and Hidden Realm, Gold Lieutenant of the Forehelien Charge and Guardian Gatekeeper of Portland, was worthy of the Ascension, once his mother's rule had come to a close.

Julia, for her part, had made assertions to the most elite members of the Order that she had no intention of abdication at any point in the foreseeable future. An assertion that Derek was happy to hear. While his future was being discussed at length behind closed doors and in whispered tones by others, he had never been asked if he *wanted* the job. He knew it was his mother's dream for him to follow in her footsteps to not only become the leader of the House of Silver, but also the entire supernatural world, but was it his dream? It was only a few years ago that his aspirations were minuscule compared to what lay before him now.

Back then, he was a trained artist who used the human body as his canvas. He was a small business owner who lived a mostly satisfying life of basic human bliss until a run-in with a succubus named Daria changed everything. After that encounter, the former orphan discovered his mother, and his home, and uncovered deeper feelings for the woman that he called his best friend. He thought of himself more as an advisor, soldier, and friend, and never once gave any thought to being a ruler, until now. While he was momentarily honored that the Order had given their blessing for his Ascension, his only outstanding thought at this exact moment was the excitement he felt for his up-coming marriage to the love of his life, Siobhan.

Siobhan's thoughts were another story. While she was making a valiant attempt to become more accustomed to the pomp and fanfare that surrounded her fiancé, she didn't really relish the idea of always being the center of everyone's attention. As time went on and the more she thought about it, she wished their life was a little more quiet. She had no reservations about being Derek's right hand as he guarded Portland or even a human ally for the Hidden, but she was unsure of the life of a Sovereign.

She watched Julia age twenty years in the past two. At times, it was all too much to think about. There were nights she lay next to him, listening to his soft snoring, wondering if either of them were ready for what was ahead. Her mind would get away with her and suddenly, images and thoughts raced through it so fast that she would begin to panic. She would think of the unlikeliest scenarios.

What else was out in the Hidden? A year ago, no one knew the Kiada was still alive. What if there was something more dangerous around the bend? What possible powers could they have?

Her brain quickly posed questions that were more real and scarier.

What if Derek were killed in the battle with the Changelings? What would become of her? The people in the Hidden had become her family, would they still feel the same? What if Julia died? Derek would be thrust onto the throne and she didn't think he was ready yet. What if they had a child? Would she be forced to make the same decision as Julia and allow him to be sent away for a chance at a normal life?

She fought hard to keep those ideas at bay. Focusing only on how thrilled she was to be spending the rest of her life with him seemed to be the only antidote for the poisonous thoughts that invaded her.

Derek sat their small suitcase on the bed, "Here we are."

"So, remind me again why we packed all of our things to come here when we are going back to Portland tonight?" Siobhan asked, her tone of voice clearly irked.

"Because," he turned to her and wrapped his muscular arms around her waist, "You and my mom have to finalize some details for the wedding and I have a Charge meeting...might be easier to just get ready here."

"Then back home for one last party," she sighed.

"Not just any party," he teased her, "*The* party to end all parties."

He started to kiss her forehead between each word.

"Then...one...more...night...until...the...big...day," Derek guffawed between each kiss as she giggled wildly.

She looked up at him, trying to hide her amusement, "How do you do that? Here I am frustrated and you just make it go away...you're infuriating, sometimes."

Derek narrowed his eyes and grinned slyly, "I'm cute that's how...and you looovve me."

He bent down and began kissing her exposed neck as Siobhan cackled. A soft, one-knuckle knock came from behind them.

"I don't mean to interrupt," Casius cleared his throat.

"Hey, Casius!" Siobhan said brightly, giving the werewolf a quick kiss on the cheek.

"Hey, can I borrow your fiancé for a bit? We've got some Charge business to take care of," he smiled down at her but she could see he was tense.

"What's up?" Derek looked at his watch, "Meeting doesn't start for an hour."

Casius's eyes seemed to darken, "Vilotta's stronghold was attacked again early this morning...seems like the Changelings are out for blood again."

"Damn...I thought the truce negotiations were working," Derek sighed heavily.

"Yeah, well, I'm not sure if either side is willing to come back to the table now," Casius replied, turning back to Siobhan, "I'm sorry, Von..."

"Of course! But...you better have him at James Station by seven, though," she warned. "If he doesn't show, I'm blaming you and going home to sleep in that big bed all alone."

Derek roared with laughter, "We'll be there."

He leaned down, giving her a kiss, "You take your half out of the middle anyway."

"Get out of here!" Siobhan's eyes widened with amusement, shutting the door behind the pair.

3

The high-pitched squall of Queen Vilotta's voice reverberated off every surface of Julia's office. The Fae leader was uncharacteristically emotional as she paced the floor, waving her thin arms in frustration, her delicate, iridescent cape rippling behind her. Casius and Derek slipped in the door quietly, closing it softly so as to not disrupt the meeting in progress. They took positions next to Silas, Tara Vena, and the Foreheilen Fae, Zhaar.

"An outrage!!" Vilotta flailed. "Insolent little...pests! I'll have them all bound and begging for the sweet release of death..."

"Vilotta, you must remain calm..." Julia soothed.

The Queen's pupils became cat-like, narrowing to thin slivers, "How calm would you remain, *Sovereign* if your walls were being infested with vermin? Hmm? I *will* be rid of them all!"

"Vilotta, you're talking about the genocide of a member of your own race...which, may I remind you, goes against the very foundation of the Great Treaty," Lenias Grey's bass voice bellowed from a corner.

Vilotta hissed but the elder of the Grey pack was unmoved.

"The *treaty*," the Fae Queen growled, her words dripping with derision, "Has already been broken...a thousand times over. When will you, old hound, realize that I am at war?"

The grizzled man leaned heavily on a thick walking staff. Its formerly rough edges were worn smooth and the wood looked soft like it had been polished. When standing erect, Lenias Grey could hit a peak at six foot nine inches, but age and battle had begun to cripple the old man's knees and walking had become difficult. Unlike his son's normally clean-shaven appearance, he carried a full beard of white that perfectly matched his hair.

The elder Grey narrowed his storm cloud eyes on the Fae queen, "Vilotta...I'm fully aware of *your* war...I've got every soldier we can spare fighting in the Wilds! Your belligerence and tactless displays only infuriates the Changelings more... it's a damn wonder more of your kind haven't revolted before now!"

"How dare you!" Vilotta hissed once more, sailing effortlessly toward the werewolf, meeting him eye to eye. Casius and Derek stood from their seats to get between the pair, but Lenias only grunted unphased by her threatening stance and the men backed away. Vilotta raised her angular chin to the air and looked down at the old man before backing away. "Lesser Fae sometimes have a difficult time understanding what is best for them."

"Oh, here we go," Lenias growled. "That's part of your problem, Vilotta...you can't see all Fae as equal..."

"We're going in circles," Julia said calmly. "Vilotta...I've called a meeting of the Order and full Council so you may state your case. This new attack is far more brazen than any that we've seen out of the Changelings...I think this warrants a deeper discussion."

"Yes...yes...but what in the meantime? We must act swiftly," Vilotta forcefully cackled. She was like a dog with a bone. "I want this to be over...one way or another...and I want the instigator captured."

She turned her cold eyes on Silas.

"Queen, we are doing everything we can..." he began.

Vilotta's sharp nose curled, "Oh, I'm sure you are...your precious mother. Tell me, in the times before the treaty...would you have given me her head yourself or would you make that someone else's task?"

Silas stared blankly at her.

"I want it done!" her sharp voice hanging in the air.

Julia nodded in exhausted resignation.

"I will not wait long for the Council to make their decision...if I do not get the answer I want, I *will* do what I must to put an end to this madness," Vilotta's voice ran cold as her magic dropped the temperature in the room by no less than twenty degrees. She turned on the heel of her crystalline boot, nodding at Zhaar and Lore, the Fae Librarian. Zhaar's lime-colored eyes shifted to Julia who nodded her approval. He stood shoulder to shoulder with his Queen as they vanished together. Derek shivered in the chilly air that remained.

"Well, that was quite the spectacle," Lenias Grey shook his head as he plopped himself into the faded blush armchair that faced Julia's honeyed wood desk. "That woman gets crazier with each decade."

Julia sighed, "I fear she will make good on her promise this time, old friend. We have to find a way to get the Changeling forces back to the negotiation table...we must hear their side. Silas... has Dimitri had any luck in the search for Varsa? We need whatever intel she can provide...now more than ever..."

"Unfortunately, my mother continues to be out of reach," he replied cautiously. "She's clearly hidden herself well."

Silas fought his own body to keep his emotions in check. He hated deceiving them, but that statement wasn't entirely a lie. His real threat at this moment though, was Casius. If the werewolf with the uncanny psychic ability got much closer, Silas was sure he would be caught. He had distanced himself from most of his Forehelien for months now, all to protect his father's secret. A secret that could cost Dimitri everything if found out. Silas had gotten quite good at burying his true emotions over the past months, but part of him still worried about Casius. He didn't know how well his abilities had developed and had no desire to test them.

"What of her mate? Allion..." he asked, deflecting the topic of his mother.

"Bah!" Lenias waived his hand and Tara grinned in amusement.

She appreciated the old man's candor.

"Allion still hasn't spoken," she began.

"Why, Captain, are you losing your touch?" Silas smirked.

"Hardly, Counsilor. What I mean to say is that he hasn't spoken...at all. Not since his capture," she returned his playful grin.

Casius let out a low whistle.

"He hasn't asked for anything? At all!?" Derek asked, shocked.

She turned to him, "No...nothing. He's effectively become mute."

"Which only adds to our frustration," Julia added. "Lenias, what can we do? Do your people have any kind of *sway* over the Changelings?"

The older man groaned a bit as he stood, "Nah...our ability to make the Fae uncomfortable during a moon is lost on them...besides, what we need is exactly what you said, Milady...we need the Changelings to talk to us...tell us what they need, their demands. It can't be all about some sort of supposed *freedom* they think they're missing..."

"Vilotta does keep the Lesser on a short leash, as it were," Silas offered.

"Bah!" Lenias spat, "I hate that word...*Lesser.* She's still ass hurt that some of her people went against her ten millennia ago and mated with humans... and now she's responsible for what was created. Lesser...bah. They aren't any lesser than a regular Fae...if that *librarian* was worth her salt, she'd remind her queen of it."

"Well, she can hold a grudge, that's for sure...and be that as it may, Dad, the point stands...Vilotta won't stand by and watch her territory fall...she'll be ruthless...and life for any of the mixed Fae will get worse," Casius asserted then glanced at Derek. "Including Megan...and Nerissa."

"I *won't* let that happen," Derek replied with dangerous anger. "Ever."

"It won't come to that," Julia remarked. "We will wait for the Council before we make any more plans. All the families must come to an agreement before we proceed...we must be patient and have faith."

Lenias leaned heavily on his staff as he made his way to the door, "While you're keeping the peace with that crazy bat, I'm going to have a conversation with some more level-headed types...see if I can get someone who can get me a meeting with the rebellion leaders."

He stopped in front of Derek, "Congratulations young man...I look forward to seeing that lovely bride of yours soon."

Derek nodded his thanks as he shook the older man's hand and Casius leaned toward his father.

"Who are you reaching out to, Dad?" His dark eyebrow cocking.

Lenias' lips spread into a devious grin, "Oh...not far beyond the borders."

"Be safe old friend," Julia replied as his shuffling steps became distant in the descending hallway.

"Beyond the borders?" Derek mused.

Casius rolled his eyes in exasperation, "Neutral parties...cryptids...those not signed in the Treaty nor affiliated with anyone."

"For what? I thought those people were like...well, Switzerland," Derek said.

"And they are...but Lenias has always kept allies...he's hoping if we really needed them, they would come down on our side of things.

That will be especially helpful if Vilotta doesn't get what she wants...or worse," Julia explained.

"Mom, do you really think she would exterminate an entire race of her people?" Derek asked. Casius, Silas, and Captain Vena hung on his words desperately waiting for an answer.

Julia stared at the small group of Forehelein, tears barely gracing her eyes, "I desperately hope not."

4

— · —

S everal hours later, the small neighborhood bar located just three doors down from Wild Inspiration Tattoo, Derek and Theo's studio, was packed with friends and family of the bride and groom. James Station, the setting for the night's festivities, was a typical neighborhood local watering hole. The space was deep, but narrow, had an ornate bar made of patinated wood, with room for only one bartender, and hosted eight or so round tables scattered throughout the floor. The floors themselves were worn smooth, the food was greasy, and the atmosphere friendly. Derek, Siobhan, and Theo had spent many after-closing hours in this place eating, drinking, and laughing and it felt like home. Tonight, it was as crowded as ever but every person was not just a mere patron, but a friend of Derek and Siobhan. They had all come together one final time to celebrate the couple's last hours of singlehood.

Siobhan knelt on a bar stool and looked over the mass of people. She entertained herself by watching their human friends unknowingly interact with members of the magical community. Part of her wished she could introduce everyone as their authentic selves, but she understood why she couldn't. While knowledge of the Hidden was not strictly forbidden, per se, it was understood that it was need-to-know. Even so, Vampires, Werewolves, and even Elves could pass fairly easily as humans, but it was the Fae that brought about the most amusement. While they were inherently raw magic and could perform glamours much like a Witch or Elf, it was their interpretation of the human species that was comical.

Zhaar stood with his back to the wall next to the jukebox in the far corner talking to a frequent female client of the studio. He had decided that he would keep his preferred shockingly white hair but he softened his naturally sharp features which made his eyes a little too big and his nose a little too blunt. Siobhan thought he looked like a bug that was smashed against a car windshield.

"You're going to fall off that stool," Casius' deep voice boomed over the loud rock anthem that blared through the bar's speakers. Siobhan turned to meet him face to face and it made her smile as she had never really looked at the towering Casius from this height.

"I'm fine...I'm keeping an eye on Zhaar. Is he...*flirting* with Carrie?" she pointed, referring to the beautiful blonde woman the male Fae was talking with. Casius followed her finger finding the couple and smiled wide.

"I think he is," he nodded, chuckling.

Siobhan frowned, "Can you hear what they're saying?"

Curiosity was getting the best of her.

Casius concentrated hard, focusing in on only the pair's voices, and nodded. "She asked him who does his hair. Apparently, she likes snow white."

He laughed.

"She better be careful...he'll lead her away into the Wilds and she'll never be heard from again," he cautioned in mock spookiness.

Siobhan looked at Casius with shock, "Casius!"

She saw his shoulders quake as he tried to restrain his laughter and Siobhan narrowed her eyes on him.

"Damn it.... You're an asshole," she laughed.

He took a pull from his beer and shrugged, "Hey, you're the one who falls for it."

"Everyone looks like they're having a good time, don't you think?" she asked. They paused their conversation when the pair overheard a couple walking up to the bar comment on the amount of alcohol they just watched someone consume.

"Did you see that tall guy in the corner?" the woman asked.

"Yeah..." replied her male companion. "Dude drank like an entire bottle of tequila like it was water."

"He's gonna feel that tomorrow," the woman chuckled as Siobhan noticed the man they were discussing was her friend and vampire, Luther.

Casius waited for the couple to walk away as he watched Siobhan closely before he continued.

"They do look like they're having fun," he nodded, "Except for you...what's going on?"

"Nothing," she rolled her eyes, "I just..."

She paused. "Just nerves, I guess.

"Bull...out with it," he pointed to his solar plexus indicating he could feel her emotions.

She hesitated, "Everyone just assumes that Derek is going to be the next Sovereign."

"Well, your wedding kind of marks his Ascension," he replied, shrugging.

"No!" Siobhan said angrily, "*My* wedding marks the day I marry my soul mate."

He lowered the beer bottle from his lips, "Okay...I'm feeling the tension now.... You don't want him to become the Sovereign, do you?"

Siobhan's eyes cut into her friend, "I don't know what I want...but more importantly, I don't think he does either. Everyone is so concerned with the path to the throne, what the Order thinks, what the Order says, but no one has ever *asked* him what he wants. That's what bothers me the most, I think."

Casius was quiet for a long moment as Siobhan returned to staring out at the crowd of partygoers. She couldn't quite believe that so many people had fit into the relatively intimate space. She smiled to herself again as she watched the Elf captain, Tara Vena, and her vampire boyfriend, Luther, swaying to the music together; she thought they looked to be in love.

Casius cleared his throat and finally took another drink, "Tell him not to do it."

"What?" she said, turning back to him.

He moved his body to allow someone by, facing Siobhan, "Tell him not to become Sovereign."

"Can he do that? I mean, Julia is pretty set on it...and now that the Order has given their blessing..." she began.

"So what? Look, Derek can remain the Guardian of Portland for the rest of his life, if he chooses. Right now, the balls in his court. If he doesn't want to do it, then no one can force him. And yes, while you think it's pretty shitty that the Order doesn't seem to care about what he thinks, there's nothing further from the truth actually. The Order doesn't want someone in charge whose heart isn't in it.... It's not like he's the first one to decline the offer."

"So, he could just say no? Then what happens?" she asked.

"Oh, it will pass to the next in line... Ideally, one of his offspring," he smirked at Siobhan.

It took her a minute to get the implication but when she did, she punched him firmly in the shoulder, "God, no Casius. We're nowhere near ready for that... if ever."

He laughed heartily, "I know, I know...then it would pass to another member of Silver Light House. Julia's family hasn't always been in charge...hers is just one of many. Just, think about it...let *him* think about it... Ultimately, it's a decision you'll both have to make."

Siobhan nodded.

"Now, please get off that stool like that...I'd kinda like to dance," Casius laughed.

Siobhan graciously gave Casius her hand for balance as she jumped onto the floor. He led her through the jam-packed room until he found them a small space among other revelers. Casius skillfully swung and spun her through several songs as Siobhan giggled through each new move. They stopped occasionally for Siobhan to take a pull or two from drinks that various friends had bought for her. Several times during the night, Siobhan would catch Derek's eye and smile. He would smile back and wink. She returned her own sweet gesture by putting two fingers in a 'V' shape. It was their own personal sign language; *I love you...I love you too.*

This flirtation between them continued throughout the night as they watched each other being showered with affection and attention from the jovial group of friends and family that had gathered to celebrate. Twice they were able to grab a dance with each other. But the pair knew that all eyes were on them and there were others vying for their attention. They both gave in to the demands of their friends knowing that in a matter of hours, they would have the rest of their lives together.

Siobhan was finally able to catch her breath and took a seat at a corner table with Tara and Megan. The three were entranced as they glanced across the room to watch a group of men; Luther, Silas, Derek, Theo, and Casius, slam shots of a clear liquid.

"They're gonna be sick," Megan laughed.

Tara chuckled, "Well, I don't know about the rest, but Luther's fine."

"Yeah, he is…" Megan giggled and their table erupted with laughter.

"So Tara," Siobhan said, smiling wryly, "How's it going with tall, dark, and Dracula?"

Tara spat beer, choking with laughter.

"Uhmm…good, we're good…" she replied, catching her breath, then took another pull of her bottle.

"I hear better than *good*," Megan smirked.

Tara looked surprised, "What? From who? Who are you talking to?"

"I have my ways," Megan chuckled.

"C'mon Tara, drop some tea…" Siobhan prodded her friend.

Tara blushed, "A woman doesn't kiss and tell."

"Yes, we do!" Megan laughed.

"Ok then…you go first, Kiada. How's your human…you *know*," the elf shrugged a shoulder.

"He's very, *very* …" she paused, thinking. "Adequate…is a good word, I think?"

"Oh," Tara wrinkled her nose then immediately realized Megan's meaning. "Oh!'

Megan winked at the elf and laughed, "*Very* adequate."

The women stared at Theo and as he turned, looking in their direction, they immediately averted their eyes. All three began giggling again.

"Alright, Elf….go. How adequate is the vampire?" Megan eyed her.

Tara sipped her drink. "Well...let's just say that there's something to be said for a man that doesn't get tired...and," she held her hands out on the table, about three and a half beer bottles wide, "I'm not *unsatisfied*."

Siobhan and Megan's eyes widened comically.

"Holy shit! Seriously?" Siobhan whispered hoarsely, looking again across the room at the group of men.

The women quietly stared for a moment.

"Do you think that's a vampire thing...or...?" Megan mused eyeing the table.

Tara shook her head, "No idea..."

The eyes of all three drifted to Silas when Tara shook her head again.

"Ok, bride-to-be...your turn," she playfully ordered. "Out with it...give us the details on His Highness."

Siobhan's eyes rose, landing on Derek. She watched him throw a mouthful of liquid back and wince as it burned in his broad chest. She pursed her lips, "I'm extremely happy."

"Are you serious? That's all you're giving us? I mean...look at him," Tara pointed. "He's so...*hot*."

Megan rolled with laughter.

"Well, he is...look at him! The body...the eyes...hell, even that jaw-line," Tara continued to ogle Derek. "He's got a six-pack, doesn't he?"

"More than that...he's got the dips in the hips," Megan commented slyly.

Tara choked with laughter again, "How do you know that?"

"I mean...we do *live* together...the man walks around shirtless in basketball shorts most of the time," she replied.

"Mmm, lucky girl."

Siobhan laughing, jokingly chided her friends, "Okay...you both need to stop lusting over my fiancé."

"Give it to us then," Tara prodded more.

"Alright...alright," Siobhan said quietly, leaning in, "I'll say this...Luther and Derek seem to have *a lot* in common."

Tara and Megan looked at her with mouths agape making Siobhan chuckle. She slumped back in her wooden chair, sipping her beer, pleased with herself.

Tara turned, looking at Derek from head to toe, "Well, I have a whole new respect for the Lieutenant...and good for you, my friend."

The women noticed the band of men, who had finally settled at a small group of tables near the bar, were eyeing them.

"Do you think they know we were talking about them?" Megan asked.

"Does it matter?" Tara offered in retort.

Megan laughed aloud, "Nope...not really."

***

Casius slammed the shot glass down on the bar and growled softly, "That has a bite."

"Oh, damn...what is that?" Derek coughed.

"It's called *Uchadia*," Luther laughed.

Theo, still recovering from his first drink of the clear liquid choked, "Which is...what exactly?"

"Vampire moonshine," Silas laughed out loud as he passed a third shot to each man.

"To a healthy and productive coupling!" Luther cheered, raising his glass.

Derek smiled wide and glanced in Siobhan's direction before throwing his head back once more.

"Shhh! Shhh, shhh," Silas hushed the group. "I think your ladies are talking about you."

"Man...don't eavesdrop," Casius laughed, scolding him. The group of friends put together two small tables and seated themselves around.

"What are they saying?" Theo leaned in toward Silas.

Derek laughed, "Are you sure you want to know?"

"Well, I'm curious," he shrugged.

Silas's eyes went wide, "Oh...well, they're discussing your...attributes."

"What?" Theo slurred as the last few drinks took effect.

"They're talking about how big your dick is," Luther laughed.

Theo frowned, "I'm not sure if I like that...or... maybe I do."

The table roared with laughter.

"Hey...Tara's talking now," Silas said.

Luther beamed, "Well now...I know my mate is satisfied...no worries there."

"God...I'm not listening to this," Casius rolled his eyes.

"What?" Luther eyed him, "We are mutually satisfying to each other...I can tell you that Tara is..."

"Stop...stop," Casius and Derek demanded, laughing and waving their hands in surrender.

"What?" Luther looked surprised. "The women are clearly having a discussion about us."

"Right," Casius said, "A private conversation...which your cousin is *still* listening to."

He playfully punched a smirking Silas in the shoulder, giving him a look that told the vampire *'Knock it off..'* The pair locked eyes for a split second. Usually there was a spark of familiarity when he touched someone he knew as intimately as his fellow Forehelien. But this time, there was nothing. It was almost like radio static and darkness. Casius frowned at his friend and stared at Silas a few more confused moments.

"Well, if they can dish about us," Theo burped, interrupting his thought, "Then isn't it fair to do the same about them?" He was becoming more inebriated as the minutes ticked by.

"Hey...dummy... You aren't dealing with average women here...Of everyone in this bar right now, those three are the most dangerous in here. I'm not touching that..." Casius replied.

"What does that mean?" Theo asked, looking in Derek's direction.

Derek slapped his buddy on the back, laughing, "It means if any of them caught us talking about our sex life with each other... we're dead men."

The table erupted in laughter once more.

It was around two in the morning when Derek made his way back to Siobhan through the gradually diminishing crowd.

"Hey, beautiful," he whispered in her ear.

The timbre of his voice sent a chill of pleasure down her back and she turned around, "Hey yourself."

She reached out and wrapped her arms around his waist to steady herself as she was feeling the effects of one too many adult beverages. He too, feeling a little inebriated, but not at his limit, bent down and gave her a quick kiss on the lips. They tasted like beer and bourbon.

"I'm going to run over to the shop and pick up a flash I drew up for Silas. I'll be right back...you good here?" he asked.

Siobhan looked around the room, "Yeah, I'm good. I've not had a good visit with Saracin yet. I know she's been on guard duty at the stronghold and just want to talk to her before she heads out...you go. I'll wait for you."

"Sounds good! I'll just be a few minutes...when I get back, we'll head back to the house," he kissed her again.

"Or…" her voice turned sultry, "We could sneak back to Arvendon and have a practice honeymoon."

He cocked an eyebrow, "What about our deal?"

"I think that practice makes perfect…if we want a perfect honeymoon," she shrugged her shoulders.

It only took Derek a second to consider her offer, "Oh, well… that's a good plan, Miles…don't go anywhere, I'll be right back."

He gave her one last kiss then turned and jogged out of the door. Siobhan made her way over to Saracin to thank her friend for coming and apologized for not being able to talk with her longer. As the elf excused herself to return to Arvendon, Siobhan sat at a table with Tara, Luther, Silas and Casius. The five finished their drinks they had on the table and ordered another round. The partiers around them began to dissipate even more and the room became noticeably quieter.

Luther raised his glass in a toast, "To the lovely bride! May you have several lifetimes of happiness."

"Here! Here!" the table said in unison.

"My turn," Silas began as he stood. "It's no secret that you and I got off to a less than hospitable start…"

"I thought you were a smarmy, asshole with a big mouth," Siobhan interrupted and the table erupted in laughter.

"Yes, yes," Silas chuckled, "But you have proven my attitude about your kind was wrong and incredibly unwarranted. Congratulations, my sister!"

Cheers, and the banging of glasses on the table echoed in the now mostly empty room.

"Thank you all for everything. I couldn't ask for a better…family," she blushed.

Right then the bartender cried out, "Last call!"

"Oo! Time for one more," Casius said as he walked to the bar to get the table one last round.

The friends sat for a while longer, finishing their drinks, relaxing, and reminiscing about shared adventures. The feeling around the table was peaceful and warm. There was no talk of Changelings or Vilotta or war. It was a happiness that couldn't be bottled and sold; it was organic and natural and he way life should always be. After what only seemed like a few minutes, Siobhan looked up at the clock on the wall, her head swimming from too much beer. She squinted her eyes to focus and nearly gasped when she saw the time.

"It's already three," she stated.

"Hey Von," the bartender said.

She looked in his direction, "Yeah Sam?" The words coming out a little slurred.

"I'm going to have to lock up... You all ready to head out?" he asked.

"Oh, yeah, sorry Sam," she apologized.

Sam laughed and shrugged, "No problem...I'd give you a key, but the city frowns on that."

Siobhan's reaction was preoccupied with her sudden realization that Derek hadn't come back from his short trip to the studio. She turned around in her chair thinking that she had somehow missed him coming back inside, but the bar was empty except for their group at the table. Frowning, she looked out of the window of the wood-framed door.

"What are you doing?" Casius called from the table as they all stood to leave.

"He didn't come back," she said to herself.

"Who didn't come back?" Luther bellowed from the table.

Siobhan turned to face the small group as they walked behind her, "Derek. He left an hour ago... he didn't come back."

5

"He's probably passed out inside," Luther suggested soberly as he allowed the heavy door to James Station to shut behind him.

The five walked toward the black door of Wild Inspiration in search for Derek. He promised Siobhan he would be back within minutes but an hour later he hadn't returned to the bar a quarter of a block away from the studio's doors.

Siobhan reached for the door handle clumsily and it swung open wide. She was doing her best to will herself into sobriety with each step. The bell on the door chimed as she crossed the threshold into the dark entryway. She made her way around the front counter, following its left curve to the wall where the light switch panel was located. Even drunk, she knew this path like no other. She flicked the three tabs up and the soft humming of the overhead lights were heard as the room brightened.

"Derek? Where are you?" she called out as she walked toward his office. Luther and Silas simultaneously grabbed both of her arms, holding her back.

"No!" Luther commanded and they heard a low growl begin to emanate from Casius.

"What?" What's wrong?" Tara whispered, reaching behind her back to pull out her concealed Glock.

Casius sniffed the air, "Someone else was here."

Luther, still holding on to Siobhan's arm, raised his chin in the direction of the office, "Silas?"

With a swift movement of air, Silas entered the room and was back in seconds. He shook his head, "No one's here."

"What?" Siobhan exclaimed. "Derek should be here, he said he was getting something for you and he would be right back!"

She shook off Luther's hold, charging to the back room to find it empty. Turning and still calling his name, she made her way into Theo's office next to also find it empty. With the rest of the group in tow, she made her way to the back door of the studio that led to the alley behind the block of buildings and pushed the heavy fire door open. It was also unlocked.

"I smell blood," Luther stated firmly.

"Me too," Silas replied concerned as the two Vampires moved around the immediate area attempting to find the source. They came upon several large droplets of fresh crimson six feet from the back door.

"He was here," Silas confirmed as he bent closer to them.

Siobhan's eyes widened, "That's Derek's blood? Then where is he?"

Her voice was building with panic as Casius bent down so he could look at her face to face, "Von. You need to breathe...we'll find him."

He did his best to assure her.

Tears welled in her eyes as she focused on his face and she knew the remnants of the alcohol had heightened her emotions, "Casius, where is he?!"

He looked to Luther and Silas, both men just returning from a trip around the block. They shook their heads; Derek was nowhere to be found. He glanced over at Tara who was on her cell phone.

"Thanks, Theo...no, I'll let you know," she said into the microphone. She disconnected the call and also looked at Casius, shaking her head. His gaze returned to Siobhan's face; her eyes closing as the tears streamed like two rivers to her chin.

"He's not at home, is he?" she whispered, her voice breaking in her throat.

"No," he replied softly.

Siobhan wanted to scream. She wanted to let out all the pain and anger she always seemed to hold just under the surface. She didn't know what happened to Derek, but she knew it had to have something to do with the Hidden. In the last few years, they had made enough enemies for a lifetime and it seemed as though they were always lying in wait for the right time to attack. They had been celebrating again. A little over a year ago, it was his commission as a Forehelien officer, now it was their upcoming nuptials. Their *wedding*. They were supposed to be married in thirty-six hours. Rage filled her as she saw their future slipping away. She held onto that fury because she knew she would need it to push her to do what she had to do. The rivers of tears stopped and Siobhan took a deep breath. Casius could see the muscles in her jaw clenching until they set.

Siobhan opened her deep green eyes, looking at Casius hard, "Looks like we're going back to Arvendon."

6

— ◦ —

T he group was quiet as they entered Her Lady Sovereign Julia of Silver Light's office in the wee hours of the morning. Tara had sent a lady-in-waiting, Ceri, to wake the Sovereign and bring her to the working chamber and no one spoke as they waited for her arrival. Siobhan sat motionless in a blush-toned wing-back chair in the corner of the room. Silas and Luther stiffened as they heard Julia approach from the hallway.

"Oh...Casius...Luther...Silas...what's going on?" Julia mused sleepily. It was then she noticed Siobhan sitting in the corner, her eyes were still red from unfallen tears.

"Siobhan! What are you doing here?" she looked around, "Where is Derek?"

Tara stepped forward, "Sovereign, that's why we're here...the lieutenant is missing."

Julia's gait faltered and she grabbed onto her desk for balance. Silas and Luther rushed to her side for support.

"I'm fine," she choked a moment. "What do you mean...Derek...my son... is missing? How?"

Casius glanced over at Siobhan expecting her to speak, but she never moved and seemed to become more distant as the seconds ticked by.

He cleared his throat as he pulled his eyes from her and looked again at Julia.

"We aren't sure, your Sovereign.... looks like he was taken from his business...maybe an hour ago," he replied.

Julia sat quietly for a few moments.

"Could it be the rogue Changelings?" she asked softly.

"Ma'am, at this point anything is possible...We've got a team searching the area for clues," Tara replied. "Have there been any updates from the Wilds? Has Elre's team made it back yet?"

Julia shook her head as a knock came from the door. Casius crossed the room, opening the door to find Alder and his wife, Jaudon, in the hallway.

"Brother," Casius sighed.

"Is it true?" Alder asked as Casius allowed them to pass.

"Yeah," he said softly.

"How is Siobhan?" Jaudon whispered.

Casius motioned with his chin to the corner of the room, "See for yourself...she's not said a word."

"Casius, she's in shock," his sister-in-law observed as the trio moved to where Julia rose from her seat.

"Alder, Jaudon...thank you for being here. I assume Tara has filled you in?" she asked.

The female werewolf nodded as she took a chair across from Julia's desk.

"Yes...I've been in contact with the Known authorities. They can't do anything until he's been missing twenty-four hours. But luckily we don't have the same red tape here, as they say," Jaudon replied.

Julia nodded her head, "Yes...Alder, Tara...who can we spare?"

They looked at each other from across the room.

Tara spoke first, her face grim, "As you know, everyone is spread thin, your Sovereign. We've moved most of our Brethren battalions to the Wilds to assist Vilotta. We're doing our best to keep the Changeling issue there so it doesn't spread to other territories. Of the Forehelien…"

"The Forehelien are also doing their best, ma'am," Alder interjected. "We have at least two members with every battalion, and the rest are stationed here, the majority in this room."

Julia nodded again but didn't speak. Siobhan blinked her dry eyes as she listened to the exchange going on around her. The anger boiled inside her, just under her skin. What she heard was there wouldn't be anyone to look for Derek. After all he had done and sacrificed for this place and now he would essentially be left to save himself, if he was even still alive.

'Don't think like that…' she said to herself.

The conversation around her turned into just droning sounds as the group discussed options in the search for Derek. Siobhan couldn't concentrate on only one voice as the noise had become overwhelming to her. She just wanted to scream at the top of her lungs right before she ripped the world apart.

She would rip the world apart looking for him herself.

As everyone rose to leave, the voices and words began to make their way into her ears again.

"We will do our best to gather everyone we can to find him," she heard Tara say.

"Julia, will you let Alder or me know if you need anything?" Jaudon added.

Siobhan felt numb and disconnected as she rose with everyone else to leave. She trailed behind the group until she heard Julia call her name. Everyone stopped at the door and waited with pregnant apprehension. Siobhan turned slightly, looking blankly at the older woman.

"Child, are you alright? Would you like to stay and talk?" Julia asked, her voice motherly and soft.

Siobhan only stared emotionless at her for another moment, then she turned, walked through the group, and left the room.

7

— · —

Siobhan marched with purpose to her and Derek's suite in the stronghold. As she turned to open the door, she heard her name being called behind her.

"Siobhan! Von, wait!" Casius yelled after her.

She ignored his words and entered her bedroom, slamming the door behind herself.

"Von," Casius said as he knocked lightly on the door, opening it. He watched her for a few minutes as she dug through the chest of drawers, pulling out a pair of jeans, tee-shirt, and socks. He waited as she took the items to the bathroom and returned a few moments later redressed and with her long auburn hair pulled into a high ponytail. She flopped herself onto the bed and laced on her black combat boots.

"So...this is what you're doing. You're not gonna talk and I just have to feel all the emotion?" he asked.

She glared at him.

"Oh, yeah, loud and clear," he replied. "Von, you have to let this out...what are you thinking right now?"

Siobhan reached into a lower drawer of the same chest, pulled out a black leather shoulder holster, strapping it on. Reaching under the bed, she found the Glock nineteen that Derek kept hidden there and shoved it into place along with extra magazines. She walked around Casius to a closet, retrieving her leather biker's jacket. When she turned around, she found Casius standing in her way. She never looked up into his face, but stared at his wide chest.

"I'm not moving until you talk to me," he said gently.

Siobhan stepped to the side and Casius moved to block her again.

"I'm serious, Von. Whatever you're thinking, don't do it," he said.

She tried to step around him again and he blocked her once more. Siobhan let out a frustrated huff and continued staring at his chest.

"If you think you can go after who took him, you're wrong. We don't even know *who* did it...I know you think what you're doing is right...but you're not in the right headspace. Please let us take care of this," he begged.

Siobhan finally looked up at him as she threw her shoulder into his solar plexus, shoving past him. She picked up her purse, rifling through it to find her identification and keys. She shoved the items in her pockets and turned to leave. Again, Casius stood between her and her goal. Her frustration at him reached its boiling point and she couldn't hang on to her cool any longer. She took a small step back and threw her right fist squarely at Casius' chest.

The werewolf, who had felt her anger rising, anticipated her reaction at him and caught her fist midair in his overly large hand. He held onto it as he tried to calm her.

"Are you ready to listen?" he asked, raising an eyebrow.

She tried to pull her hand back but he wouldn't release her. She drew back her left fist and he caught that one mid-air right before it met his chin. Siobhan's face filled with rage.

"Goddamn it!! Let me go!" she howled.

"Hey! Your voice has been restored...you ready to talk?" he said.

"Fuck you, Casius!" Siobhan struggled to free her fists.

The werewolf furrowed his brow, "I don't have time right now...thanks for the offer...but one of my best friends is missing and I need to help his fiancé find him...but she's being a lunatic at the moment!"

Siobhan slowly stopped struggling and Casius dropped her hands. She stood in front of him, hanging her head low. Tears dropped from her eyes like giant raindrops as her entire body shook. Casius felt her anger shifting to sorrow before she raised her face. He took a step forward and enveloped her entire body in his arms. He held her tightly and allowed her to bury her face in his chest and cry violently. The aura of pain that flowed off her was emotionally overwhelming for him, bringing tears to his own eyes, but he held onto her and fought through the waves of grief.

After several minutes, he felt a tiny bit of her tension release and she withdrew from his embrace. Siobhan wiped at her face and coughed as her sobbing eased. She felt embarrassed and sad, but not as uncontrollably angry as she did a moment before. She stood with Casius still holding onto her shoulders in comfort for a little while longer.

"You okay?" he asked softly.

She nodded.

"Hey, no going back to silence...I need you to talk to me," he prodded.

Siobhan sighed, "I don't know what to say—"

"Say anything! Tell me what you're thinking right now...tell me how pissed off you are...just don't shut me out," he bent down to look into her tired eyes.

She nodded again, sitting on the edge of the bed as Casius took the seat across from her.

"I have to go after him, Casius. No one else is going to..." she began.

"That's not true! Were you even listening in there? They're all doing what they can to find him."

He paused, "We *will* find him, Von."

"No, the Brethren and Forehelien are at their limit right now. I know that...you know that. It's up to me...I can't ask any of you to pull out of the fight in the Wilds," she said.

"You can't do this on your own," Casius countered.

"I'll do what I have to."

"Not alone you're not...if you're determined to do this, I'm coming along," he interjected.

"Casius, I can't ask you to leave your post here," Siobhan replied.

He leaned close to her, "I didn't hear you ask...I'm telling you what's happening. My brother and the rest have Arvendon covered...and we will have at least one Brethren team in the field with us. Looks like you have a choice, my friend. You sit this out...or...you've got a partner," a sly smile formed in the corner of his mouth. "What'll it be?"

Siobhan quietly considered him for a moment before she replied, "Let's find my fiancé... partner."

8

Chateau de Blanche was tucked serenely into a sheltered valley at the foothills of the French Pyrenees. Surrounded by giant trees of English oak, Sweet chestnut, and pine, the grounds of the enormous fifteenth-century edifice were secluded and quiet. Looking picturesque and like it was made from a fairy tale, Silas's home now felt dark and daunting.

His footsteps echoed off the stone walls of the chateau, his pace quickening as he made his way through the winding hallways. Silas could walk these corridors in the dark, while sleeping, and be heavily drunk, if he had to. He was born here and spent his entire childhood watching the seasons pass from their dabs and arrow slits. He loved his home, but in the past several months Silas hated returning to this place of solace.

Now, the pit in his gut grew by the minute as he took the final turn into this father's study. Approaching the ornate beech door, Silas knocked once before entering. He knew his father had already heard him coming, so there was no pretense of politeness.

Dimitri Montagne Blanche sat stoically behind a large oak desk. His larger-than-life presence seemed to tower over everything in the room. He never glanced up at Silas as he entered, but slowly swirled the semi-clear liquid in his glass.

"You looked troubled, *mon gars*," Dimitri said thickly.

Silas sighed. He knew how the conversation was already going to go. He had been here, in this same study over the past year more than fifty times having the same tiring discussion. The first dozen times it felt like Deja vu but now it was more like a rerun on basic cable. And since there had never been a television in this castle, this repeated exchange was the only thing on.

"Father...we have to talk," he stated as a matter of fact. Meeting Silas's eyes, Dimitri finally looked up from his glass.

"No...no we do not," his voice heavy with his native French.

"*Merde!*" Silas hit the desk with his fist, cursing. Dimitri's eyes widened angrily at his son.

Slamming his own fist, his yell filled the room, "I have said my peace with this!"

"The Fae?! Yes, Father...let us talk about the Fae. Their people have revolted against their own queen because of *her*. This is not just about what is best for *our* people...we have to think about what is best for everyone!" Silas charged.

"Everyone...Elves, Fae...us. The Order. We are safer while she is here!" Dimitri rebutted.

Silas started to pace around the study. Concentrating on one of a thousand titles of books that filled the shelves, he worked to control his emotions. He had read every one of the books in this room over the past three hundred years; some many times over. He was desperate to fall into one of their stories right now.

Silas shook his head, "This is not working, Father. We must act! We need to do what is right and hand her over to the Forehelien...we can keep her—"

"Yes! Yes...what a wonderful job the Forehelien did keeping her behind bars before, *fantastique!*" Dimitri finished his drink, laughing.

"No...no one knows she is here....if no one knows she is here...no one can try another rescue attempt."

Silas growling in frustration, threw his hands in the air, "Vilotta wants her head! Don't you understand!? She will stop at nothing until she gets it!"

Dimitri flinched. It was a reaction that Silas wasn't expecting and he stood staring at him for a long moment.

"Father, Vilotta holds Varsa directly responsible for the Changeling incursion...they are running rampant in the Wilds...and now..." Silas hung his head.

Sitting his glass down slowly, Dimitri's face filled with questions, "What has happened?"

"What does it matter? Do you even care that the Sovereign's son is missing? Taken from his own Komma," he snarled.

"No...no..." Dimitri said, shaking his head wildly, "That cannot be...how is Julia? His *l' amie?*" Dimitri's voice quickly filled with concern as he spoke of Siobhan.

"Shock. Despair. Anger...everything you would expect," Silas paused. "Father...Vilotta is talking of destroying her own kind...we cannot keep Varsa here...she must face justice."

Dimitri returned to his chair, pouring himself another drink, "Take what guards you must to help with the search for Derek...we will help where we can...whatever Julia needs is at her disposal."

Even though it shouldn't have surprised him, Silas still stared at his father in shock. Just like that, the conversation about Varsa was over. She would rot away in a cell in the lower dungeon of Chateau de Blanche for eternity. Angry and defeated again, Silas turned on his heel, charging out of the room.

9

—·—

Casius jumped from his seat, "Alright! That's what I'm talking about."

"Where do we start?" Siobhan asked.

"What does your gut tell you?" he replied.

She thought for a moment. While they had made a quick look around the studio, nobody really searched for any clues as to what may have happened; after all, they had been drinking a bit and she knew *her* head was fuzzy at the time. She also knew there was a small group of Brethren canvassing the area downtown.

"We should take a look at the office first...then meet with the group on the ground," she replied.

"That was my thought. You ready for this?" he eyed her.

Siobhan nodded and led the way out of the room. They made their way back to the Sovereign's chamber to use the doorway back to Derek's office in Portland and ran into Alder and Luther.

"Hey," Alder stopped his brother, "Where are you two going?"

Casius pulled his brother to the side, motioning to Siobhan to go ahead. She complied as the men watched her.

"We're going back to Portland to assist with the search," he told his brother.

"Why?" Alder asked, his tone accusatory.

Casius furrowed his brow, "Why? Because a member of the Forehe-lien...the Sovereign's *son* is missing. Isn't that a good enough reason?"

"Or," Alder lowered his voice, "Is it because you have feelings you need to work out?"

"You can't be serious?" he laughed.

"I think someone else should head up the search in Portland," Alder suggested.

Casius couldn't believe what he was hearing, "Who would you suggest, brother? Silas?"

He looked around for the vampire.

"Exactly *where* is Silas? Looks to me he's pulled another disappear-ing act," he hissed.

"I think you're too close, brother," Alder snapped. "I know how you feel about her."

"You clearly wouldn't know your own ass if it was handed to you," Casius fumed indignantly.

Alder begged hoarsely, "Then tell me, Casius. Tell me you aren't in love with her...because from where I stand, you two are rather close."

"You have no idea what you're talking about! I'm warning you, Alder...keep your tongue..." Casius growled as he shoved his brother against the frame of the door. The two felt the familiar swift move-ment of air as Luther appeared next to them.

"Gentlemen...do we have a problem?" he asked the pair, his eyes bouncing between them both.

"Nope, just an older brother who doesn't know when to quit," Casius gave Alder one last shove.

"You're proving my point, little brother..." Alder snapped.

Casius laughed sardonically, "You *really* need to shut up."

He turned to leave when Alder grabbed his arm, "I saw you two...not twenty minutes ago in her room..."

Casius turned back, "I don't know what you *think* was going on...but she just lost her mate. She's dying inside... I'm being a good friend."

"Are you sure? Or are you looking for an opportunity—" Alder snarled until Casius's fist met his brother's jaw. Lunging, Luther put himself between the brothers, holding Casius at bay.

"I told you to shut your mouth, Alder! Goddamn it! I can't believe you would think I would be so...dishonorable. You can go to hell, brother," Casius flung the door wide, disappearing into the portal. As he swung the door open from the other side, he found Siobhan searching Derek's desk.

"Jesus, Casius!" she startled.

"Sorry," he apologized.

She eyed him, "Everything okay with you and Alder?"

"Oh, yeah...we're good now..." he lied. "You find anything?"

Siobhan shook her head, "Not really...I did find this flash under the desk."

She handed him a white sheet of paper with a shield covered by crossed swords. The blade on the left side read 'Ex sanguines', while the other simply read 'Vita'. Five stars surrounded the shield and blades to round out the artwork.

"Ex sanguines vita," he read out loud softly.

Siobhan shrugged, "Sanguines...like, sanguine? As in blood?"

"It means 'Of blood life'. This part here," he pointed to the shield and swords, "Is a Vampire family crest...specifically, The Montague Blanche family."

"This is what Derek was coming for when he left the party...he had to be in here, right?" Siobhan's voice vibrated.

Casius nodded, "I mean...yeah, we can assume that...but nothing else looks out of place."

"He's always been tidy...and fairly minimalist," she glanced around the room looking for anything else askew. Casius made his way out of Derek's office and began searching around adjoining rooms. Siobhan followed close behind as the pair looked for anything that may be missing or out of sorts. It wasn't until they entered the third, and final, procedure room that they found what they were looking for.

It wasn't anything that Casius would have noticed himself, but something that Siobhan honed in on immediately. The room was neatly kept with a small number of unopened supplies sitting organized in several clear plastic bins with drawers on a short counter space lining the left wall. There was just a small gap between the edge of the counter and the back wall where Siobhan saw something shiny on the floor. She walked around the tattoo table, moving the metal-wheeled work tray out of her way, and bent to pick the items off the floor.

"What are those?" Casius asked.

Siobhan rolled them in her fingers, "They're lining needles...on the floor. I didn't notice them before."

She looked further into the narrow space. Reaching her arm all the way to her shoulder, she retrieved a small square box that looked to Casius to hold more of the thin metal pieces. Siobhan shook her head.

"Something's wrong...These aren't even kept on this end of the counter...as a matter of fact..." her voice trailed off as she threw open the cabinets. What she found sent a chill down her spine as she saw what looked like a rush to clean up a struggle. The entirety of the supplies looked thrown in all directions in the hollows of the built-in storage cupboard.

"So...that's the secret? Just shut the door and no one sees the mess?" Casius asked lightly.

Siobhan shook her head, "No...no Casius...this isn't how this was left. I would never store supplies like this...this looks like someone trying to clean up in a hurry."

"Could one of your employees have been in a rush to get to the party?" he offered.

"Absolutely not," she replied firmly, pulling out a plastic case that matched what sat on the countertop. "This is what we keep those needles in...and it goes here."

She sat it in an empty spot on the Formica counter.

"Someone's been in here," she assured him. "And cleaned up fast."

Casius nodded his head, "Okay...so, Derek comes in the front door and directly to his office. He hears something in this room and comes to check it out...but he's been drinking, so maybe his reflexes aren't what they should be."

"Sounds reasonable, keep going," she pushed.

"He finds someone in here...they struggle...make a mess...somehow they get Derek out of the back door, into the alley. But how...and why?" he mused, pacing around the room.

"The only blood we've found so far was outside, right? No blood in here or in the hallway. They could have had a weapon on him and he walked outside." Siobhan thought aloud.

"That's pretty good. After he's out there...maybe there's another struggle and he gets hit over the head." Casius continued and then paused to look at Siobhan. She had her eyes closed and looked to be pushing back tears.

"Hey," he touched her arm, "I'm sorry...I didn't mean to."

She looked up at him, her face firm, "No, it's okay...I need...*we* need to keep going."

"Okay," he started over, "So, he hears someone, they get the jump on him...they go outside...they knock him out...then before they leave, make sure everything looks as it's supposed to be...? Does that sound right?"

She looked around, "If they took him, why would they care if we noticed a struggle in a random room?"

Casius paused for a moment, "To throw us off? Maybe they expected just Theo to come looking...or you. Buy more time to get away?"

"Maybe." she wondered out loud. "Let's find the Brethren group...maybe they've heard something."

Siobhan locked the doors to the studio and the pair made their way toward James Station. From there, they walked another two blocks before taking a left down a side street. It was seven o'clock in the morning and the city was just starting to fully wake. The sky had just begun to lighten from violet blue to shades of orange. Birds that had made nests for the summer in the crooks and corners of buildings were just starting to sing in the burgeoning daylight. The pair walked another three blocks before they met up with the group of Brethren infantry that had canvassed the area.

"What'd you hear?" Casius asked the officer in charge; a young, thin Werewolf by the name of Henric.

"We've been in every grocery, bar, and diner in a ten-mile radius...we've only had one lead," Henric explained.

"Don't hold back man," Casius prodded.

"Old, black van, no tags...was seen hauling ass out of the alley around two-thirty. Asked the witness if they saw a driver, he did...but all we got was a male," he replied.

"Which direction were they headed?" Siobhan prompted harder.

Henric pointed, "Turned east. We concentrated up and down that stretch...only got a couple of humans that *might* have seen the black van."

"Where was your last witness that saw it?" Casius asked.

Henric pulled up the map on his phone and pointed three miles to a cross street, "Here. Grand and Macon...after that...nothing."

"Good work, we'll take over...you guys head back and get some rest," Casius ordered.

"Yes sir," the young man replied and the group jogged back toward the studio.

Siobhan turned to Casius as they began walking toward the corner on the map, "How are they getting back to Arvendon?"

"They aren't...they'll go to one of the safe houses and stay until needed," he replied.

The pair walked in silence for the next twenty minutes. Around them, the city was coming alive with people and sound as the daily routines of the residents of Portland began once more. As they got closer to the intersection, Casius noticed that it seemed somewhat deserted. He wondered who Henric's team could have spoken to at that time of night when there wasn't much going on. They continued to survey each building until they came to an exceptionally narrow alley. Casius felt a dark aura emanating from the access, and couldn't help but to be drawn into it. The realization of what he was feeling hit him instantaneously and like a ton of bricks: he was looking into something he never expected. He grabbed Siobhan's arm before she could enter the alleyway.

"No! Stop!" he whispered harshly. Casius closed his eyes and focused on the energy. He could feel the rhythmic pulsing as the anomaly breathed with its own life. But it was slow and gentle, almost as if it were asleep. He opened his eyes to see her staring at him.

"What is it?" Siobhan asked.

Casius shook his head, "Nowhere we should be...we need to leave."

"Casius...if Derek is down there—" she protested.

"No, Von…we need backup if we go in there," he warned. "We'll come back…we're going to need a plan before setting off half-cocked."

Siobhan eyed him for a moment before agreeing to regroup and return. They walked several blocks back to the studio when she dared to ask the question burning inside her.

"What's down that alley, Casius?"

He sighed heavily because he knew she wouldn't let it go, "It's a dark portal. It's a lot like the doorways that we use to move in and out of the Hidden…except a dark portal has its own energy…almost like a living burglar alarm."

"Where does it go?" she asked.

"They are like any doorway…but they almost always open into a dark grove," he shrugged.

"Which is…?" She asked impatiently. She hated grilling him.

Casius stopped walking and rubbed his large hand over his face, "Rogue territory."

10

The pair rounded the corner onto Park Street and back to the Wild Inspiration. Siobhan was still reeling from what Casius had told her.

"So...this Dark Grove...Rogues are just...living there?" she asked.

"Yeah...I mean, they're on the run...and there are *a lot* of dark groves," he replied.

Siobhan used her key, opening the door, "So, why don't the Brethren and Forehelien you know...arrest people living there? They're all wanted, right?"

"Oh yeah, but portals and the groves themselves aren't exactly like the Hidden. The rogues that create those doorways also design their own sort of alarm system to keep us out...and that's *if* we find one. There are whole teams of Brethren that just search for the dark portals...or I should say there were. Most of them are in Fae lands now. That portal in the alley? Is *huge*...we can't just go charging in...I've seen them rigged to collapse on themselves," explained Casius.

"Dark magic, dark portal...leads to dark groves. What are they like?" She opened the small refrigerator that sat under the reception desk and pulled out two bottles of water, tossing one at Casius.

He shrugged, cracking open the top, "I mean...pretty typical of any place you want to avoid...and no one can be trusted."

"I guess not," Siobhan muttered and collapsed on the sofa in the waiting area.

He watched her for a long moment, "You need sleep. Let me take you home so you can rest.."

"No...I'm not going anywhere. I'll be fine," she protested.

"Von..."

"I said no Casius!" Her voice tinged with anger.

He sighed, sitting on the couch across from her, "Alright...but we can't stay here. Don't you have to open today?"

She hung her head.

"Right...the wedding tomorrow," he said softly.

"Well, that's not gonna happen. So, we need to make a plan to go into that portal tonight," she continued bitterly.

"Von...we can't go in and purposely cause trouble. You need to understand, these people are dangerous and you...well, you stick out like a sore thumb," he said.

"What are you saying? We're not going after Derek?" she countered.

"Von...we don't even know he's there. It may be just a coincidence that we found that doorway," he tried to dissuade her but even he didn't even believe it himself.

She cocked an eyebrow at him, "You seriously think that?"

He let out a short huff of breath, "No."

"You realize if you don't show me how to access that portal, I'll figure it out on my own, right?" she stared at him.

Casius rolled his large eyes, "Damn it...yeah, I know....Fine. We'll go, but I have two conditions.."

"Casius..."

"Two conditions," he emphasized, "First, you have to try to get some rest."

"Fine. Your second?" her voice suddenly exhausted.

"While we're there, you follow *my* lead...without question. These people won't hesitate to kill. Please...promise me," his voice was somber, but commanding. Siobhan knew that he was right, she would need him to navigate them safely through the area, so she agreed.

"I can do that," she nodded. "But, I'm not going home Casius...I...I can't. I won't sleep in that bed until he comes home."

Siobhan's voice shook and he was worried she would break down again.

"Hey...hey, it's okay...you don't have to...we can lay low here," he reached out, touching her hand.

She nodded again, laying back on the worn sofa. Casius watched her close her eyes and heard her breathing slow. He sat quietly for an hour before he decided to take a quick trip back to Arvendon to get ready for their mission tonight. He was worried about the journey in general, but to take a human along, especially one as well-known as her, would top off the riskiness gauge. Siobhan would need a disguise. A damn good one.

11

The hammers in his head were beating fiercely against the inside of his skull. He dared not even open his eyes for fear that if any light hit them, his temples would actually explode. So he kept them shut and instead, focused on the rest of the sensations around him. His back and palms felt like ice. He moved his hands around slowly, investigating his surroundings. He was lying down, he knew that much. Cold, rough, hard, gritty. Concrete, maybe? He touched his head.

"Ah," he winced.

Yeah, that hurt.

Derek slowly opened his lids and peered as best he could out of slits they made. The room was pitch dark and he couldn't see his hands as they touched his forehead once more. This time he felt the stiff, scab-like texture of dried blood. He opened his eyes wider and made an attempt to focus on any shapes around him, but there was only the pitch-black void.

He raised up, realizing his abdominal muscles were sore. Memory flooded his mind as he remembered being hit by some sort of bat and kicked in the ribs. Derek leaned against the wall behind him realizing it was made of cinder block. The air smelled damp but he could also make out other scents like dirt and...gasoline.

Derek waited for his eyes to adjust, but he realized he was indeed in pure darkness. He couldn't hear any sounds, not even the movement of air. Resting his head against the wall, he focused on pushing the pain from his body. He concentrated on every inhalation, then, with his exhale he forced the aches from his midsection into the stale air around him. Inhale. Exhale. Breathe in. Breathing out he quieted the thumping in the front and temples of his head, driving them into the cinderblock of the wall. After repeating the exercise for what he thought was ten or so minutes, he felt better and the discomfort had stopped. He felt well enough to stand.

Rising, he felt his way around the small space where he was being kept. He counted his steps as he walked: *seven, eight, nine, ten,* turn. He wore a size fourteen shoe so he could estimate the room was ten foot by eight foot. He realized he ran into no additional comforts such as a mattress or sink.

"Criminals are housed better than this," he muttered.

"Is that so?" a voice in the darkness replied.

12

"Sergeant Rollings, it's good to see you again," Jaudon's voluptuous lips spread into a bright, genuine smile.

"Jaudon Dromon-Grey," the stout man reached out a stubby hand, "It's been a while...about a year, right, counselor?" He opened the cheap, wooden door, allowing her to pass.

Her eyes sparkled, "Yes, I believe it has been...I don't even believe I got to thank you for all the help with the house explosion out in Pikewood...still no leads on who razed my client's house?"

Rollings grinned sheepishly, shaking his head, "No...unfortunately not."

Jaudon patted his arm flirtatiously, "Come now...he's not litigious...honestly, he's moved on and has remained pretty...*silent* on the matter...he's living a life of seclusion now. I'm here for a whole other reason."

She sat smoothly in the chair across from the sergeant in the bare interview room and crossed her shapely legs. This was not the first time they put on an act like this for anyone who may be watching. In the Known, Jaudon Grey was an exceptionally well- educated and cunning attorney. Her specialty was civil rights and her reputation as an extraordinarily skilled litigator was well-earned. Her presence could intimidate even the most grizzled cop, but when she smiled, even the coldest heart turned soft.

She used these same skills in the Hidden as well. Her ability to read, write, and speak seven languages, including ancient Vampire, made her indispensable as a translator and arbitrator among all the signed member groups of the Great Treaty. She was an expert in werewolf politics making her the clear choice to serve as the lead mediator for Grey pack. And her competence to walk seamlessly in both worlds made her a master liaison between the Known and the Hidden.

Rollings followed her fluid movement intently.

"Are we alone?" Her eyes raised toward the camera on the wall.

"Oh!" Rollings whispered. He reached for a small remote, pointed it at the camera, and its red light extinguished. He turned back to her, "What can I do for you?"

Jaudon's voice dropped to a whisper, "I'm looking for someone. Derek Argent."

"Argent!?" Rollings gasped loudly as Jaudon eyed him forcefully.

"Argent?" he questioned quietly. "What's going on?"

She shook her head, "No idea...but we need eyes on the streets. It's possible he's a hostage for the Changelings. But we still haven't received a demand nor have they claimed responsibility. He disappeared early this morning from his Komma party, looks like he was taken from the alley behind his place of business."

"Jaudon, it's not been twenty-four hours...I can't turn in a missing person's report yet...but, I might be able to pull some strings with a confidential informant, or two." He paused. "Wait. So, with Argent gone, Portland is unprotected?" Rollings asked, his voice hinting at apprehension.

"No old friend...we wouldn't let that happen. My husband will make sure nothing...*unseemingly*...happens while the Guardian is lost," she patted his hand. The sergeant's eyes widened in worry and the werewolf felt a pang of empathy for him. "I promise, Jack...we won't let anything happen to you or your wife."

"Ever since we heard about that dragon-born coming out...we've been looking over our shoulders a little more," he swallowed hard.

Jaudon nodded, "I know. But, Lenias promised your people a long time ago that we would protect you...and your secret. The old man never forgets those who helped him...or his commitments."

Jack Rollings smiled thankfully, "I appreciate that, Jaudon. I'll do what I can in getting the word out about Argent." He looked at the leather strapped watch on his wrist, "I've got to go...I got chosen for a big fraud task force."

Jaudon rose to leave, "Oh?"

"Yeah, I haven't looked at the case file yet...sounds pretty standard. Preacher bilking followers for money for *eternal salvation* or some sort of bullshit," he chuckled.

"Well, that sounds downright boring. It was good to see you, Jack," Jaudon commented in a normal voice as the pair entered the hallway. "I'll see you soon."

"Sounds good!" the Sergeant called behind her as the door clicked shut.

13

— · —

C asius closed the closet door with a soft click as he made his way back to the waiting area where Siobhan slept. He hated to disturb her peace, but knew that if she was determined to look for Derek, nothing would stop her and he refused to allow her to do it alone. He knelt beside her, shaking her gently.

"Von? Hey..." he said softly.

She startled in her seat, "Oh! Damn it..."

"Hey...sorry to scare you," Casius apologized.

"No...no. You're good," she sat up, rubbing her eyes, her head hazy from hard sleep. "How long have I been out?"

He chuckled, "Well, it's dark out...so, I'm going to say about fourteen hours."

"There's no way...I just leaned back a second ago," she threw herself off the sofa to peer through the blinds only to find the street lights on.

"Casius! Why—" she scolded him.

"Because you needed it, that's why. I was busy anyway," he replied firmly.

She returned to the sofa rubbing her eyes more, "With what?"

"A plan. We can't risk you being recognized when we go into the dark grove...so, I got some help," he nodded down the hallway behind Siobhan. She turned her head slowly to see a beautiful elf with short dark hair and a bag slung over her shoulder standing just outside Derek's office door.

"Saracin?" Siobhan said with shock.

"Hallo love," she cooed with her thick brogue.

Siobhan turned back to Casius, "Not that I'm not thrilled that she's here, but how's she going to get me into the dark grove unnoticed?"

"You need a disguise...one that can go under the magical radar, as it were," the werewolf explained.

Saracin sat on the arm of the sofa, "I can help you with that...but, we better get started before I'm missed."

"What?" Siobhan eyed the pair.

"She's helping us...discreetly," Casius sighed.

"What does that mean?" Siobhan cocked her head to the side, asking pointedly. She was getting the strong feeling that he was hiding something from her.

Casius's eyes darted between both women, "Well..."

"His brother is pissed off that he ran off to help you. Alder wants the Forehelien to regroup and hunt down whoever did this his way," Saracin interjected. Siobhan's eyes widened and she conveyed a *we're gonna talk later* look toward Casius.

"Thanks, Sari," he mumbled.

"Well," Siobhan stood, announcing to the pair, "Let's get this started then."

The tall elf led Siobhan back to Derek's office for privacy and began her work. She spent more than an hour coaxing enchantments through the air and whispering in a language that Siobhan did not understand to get the look she wanted just right. Instead of explaining as she went and talking Siobhan through the process, she would stand back, cocking an eyebrow and say "Hmmm...nope." Or "Oh, yes, that's perfect!"

When the facial features were finally complete, she placed a duffle bag at Siobhan's feet.

"Now, I've got the glamour finished. You just need to change into something a little more...elf-like," she grinned deviously. Saracin turned as Siobhan pulled garments out and dressed quickly.

After a few moments, she asked, "How do I look?"

"Badass," Saracin grinned, turning around.

"Oh! I almost forgot," Siobhan slipped her engagement ring off her finger, handing it to her friend. "Take care of this for me? If...if we don't get him back—"

"Hey," Saracin grabbed her shoulders, "You will bring him home...no worries, yeah?"

The pair of women turned and walked confidently back into the waiting room minutes later.

"I'd like to introduce Siae of the Green Court," Saracin announced to the room.

Casius looked up, "Holy shit."

Siobhan appeared nearly unrecognizable to the werewolf as Saracin's glamour almost completely transformed the human. Her round cheeks were now slimmer and her face narrow. Siobhan's ears became pointed and recognizably elf-like. Her hair color was dark black and braided along her scalp in several layers on either side to create a faux-mohawk look. Saracin added small details such as dark makeup with black eyeliner and a small scar on her right cheek. The only remnant of Siobhan that remained was the crystal green of her eyes. The entire look was completed by the costuming that included tight, black, leather pants, a fitted corset-style top and combat boots. Every detail added to her new persona's ferocity. Casius stood uncomfortably close to her, inspecting every detail. She eyed him carefully as he took a step back, smiling.

"Unbelievable. Nice work my friend," he let out a low whistle. "What's with the name?"

"Siobhan Is An Elf. Siae," she shrugged.

Casius rolled his eyes, "Clever."

"Remember...this glamour is only stable for twenty-four hours. This time tomorrow night, you'll be back to yourself," Saracin warned.

Bowing slightly to the elf, Casius thanked her, "Alright...we need to get moving. Thanks again, Sari."

"You two keep safe. I expect to hear from you soon," she replied. "Oh! I almost forgot!" Saracin handed a leather scabbard and short sword to Siobhan.

"Put this on...you can use an elf blade, yes?" she asked.

Siobhan chuckled, "Definitely...trained by the best."

"I thought so," she said smiling. "This one is kinda special."

Saracin pulled the curved blade from its sheath, revealing the sword. She offered it to Siobhan.

Siobhan grasped the hilt of the blade and nearly recoiled as it felt like ice for a moment, but quickly warmed to her touch.

"Oh?" Siobhan turned the bare blade over in her hands, eyeing the intricate scrollwork that had been tooled on the metal. For a blade, it was quite beautiful. The sword was heavy, but not overly weighted and felt surprisingly balanced.

"She's called Liars Shank Warblade...she'll keep you safe," Saracin smiled.

"I'll take good care of ...*her*," she promised.

Casius smirked as he eyed the elf, but remained silent.

"Alright! You two need to get moving...be safe...and remember...you've got about twenty-four good hours. Make the most of them," Saracin ushered them out the door, locking up behind them.

She continued to watch them on the sidewalk, whispering a blessing of good travel to the pair, "*Turas s`abhailte.*"

14

— · —

The sun had long since sank behind the horizon when the familiar footsteps of the Grey Pack leader were heard in the halls of Arvendon.

"I came as quickly as I could," Lenias Grey's voice filled the room as he hobbled heavily on his wood staff. "Sovereign, are *you* okay?"

Julia, sitting behind her desk, nodded curtly, but her watery eyes reflected the hurt in her heart. After years of being apart from her child, he was missing again. It was a desperate pain she never wanted to feel after all those years, but it came crashing on her like a tide. She opened her mouth to answer, but couldn't find the right words.

"Well, of course, you're not," the elder of the Grey pack furrowed his brow. "What do we know?" he demanded, turning to his eldest son.

"Right now, not a lot. We know the Guardian was taken from his business between two and three this morning. Brethren on the ground reported witnesses seeing a black van speeding in the area around that time." He shook his head, "Not much else."

"Who do you still have out there?" the old man asked.

"One Brethren contingent...and," Alder sighed.

"What son? Who else?" Lenias' gruff voice commanded.

"Casius."

"Good. Your brother is good on the ground—"

"Father...he's got Derek's fiancé with him...Siobhan," Alder grunted.

Lenias spat, "What? What's that boy thinking, taking that human girl with him?"

"Father...I don't think my brother is thinking clearly," he replied.

"Why is that, Alder?" Julia asked, finally finding her voice again as their exchange caught her attention.

"Sovereign, I'm sorry...but I think my brother has feelings for your son's soon-to-be wife," Alder explained cautiously.

"Boy, what are you talking about?" his father growled. Lenias was the kind of man that had no time for nonsense.

"It's no secret that he and Siobhan are close. And at first, I know it was just innocent curiosity for both of them...we're all very much like family. But, I've seen Casius spending more and more time with her in the last year. Even earlier today, I saw them in her living quarters. I just think that my brother's feelings have developed for her," he replied. "I'd like your permission, Milady, to order them from the search."

"Son, don't you think you might be reading too much into this?" Lenias offered.

"Father, you didn't see them earlier—"

"Bah!" he barked at Alder then turned to Julia, "I don't think for one second that my son's feelings are misplaced on your son's betrothed. Although, I think maybe recalling them from the search is a good idea...it's no place for a human with no abilities."

Julia took a deep breath, "Alder, I understand your concerns... albeit, misguided as they are." She turned to the older man, "I think some of this miscommunication is of my own making, Lenias. I am sorry."

"I don't understand, Milady?" Alder replied, confused.

"Remember after the bombing last year? We learned that Daria used the Asinus Profitis on Siobhan?" she began.

Alder nodded, "Yeah, the Fool's Seer spell."

"Casius was instrumental in its removal. But, Alder...what you may not understand is the bond that was formed between them," she rose from her chair, making her way to him.

"Siobhan has lived a very difficult past. The things that he had to see...and feel...in her mind...those are deeply painful and *personal* memories. Some things that I'm sure she hasn't shared *ever*...not even with my son. Things she would like to forget. Those types of memories can either invoke repulsion in people...or empathy. Your brother chose empathy. He understands the memories that she was forced to share with him while he helped heal the wound the spell made, she can't even begin to verbalize...but *he* knows them. He saw them...he felt them. In a way, he lived them with her."

"Your brother is very special...he's so much more developed psychically than any of your kind I've ever known. And *that* is very personal to *him*. I can assure you that his feelings for Siobhan are deep...but not in the way you imagine." Julia's warm hands lay on Alder's for a moment before she turned to speak to Lenias.

"As for Siobhan's abilities...all I can say is that she is tougher than she looks. The young lady can hold her own...not unlike myself when we were much more youthful, isn't that right, Alder?"

Color rushed Alder's face, "Father, I have no doubt that Siobhan can handle herself. She did best Silas not so long ago."

Lenias was quiet for a long moment. He had heard about what happened a few years ago in a boxing ring between the vampire Silas and a then unknown human woman. Since then, he had come to know Julia's son and his mate and found himself quite fond of the pair.

"Ah...well, maybe she'll do okay. I can't say I know a time when a human set out to knock a vampire down a notch...and won," he shrugged. "Besides, it won't be long until Vilotta comes beating on your door, Sovereign, demanding to be paid attention to. We need to be ready."

Lenias turned, heading for the door, "I'm going to sit in the Conclave and think for a bit...let's see who I run into."

The door snapped shut behind him leaving Alder and Julia alone. He was quiet for a moment forming his apology before turning back to her.

"I apologize, Sovereign. I meant no disrespect to you or your family with my suspicions," Alder's eyes never left the floor.

"Alder, please...I've already had my fill of formality today," she sighed, slumping on the edge of her desk.

Looking up, he stepped toward her, "Okay...then how about this. Julia, I'm sorry for what I implied...I had no idea that any of that went on. Casius never said a word... Which, I guess, only proves his actions to be honorable."

"Your brother needs you, Alder. I meant what I said...his abilities far surpass any werewolf I've met. I don't know if that will be a help or a hindrance for him," she closed her eyes trying to concentrate. Alder watched her for another moment before taking her into his arms as Julia melted in his firm hold. All the pain and sadness instantly washed over her and she began to sob.

"I can't lose him again...not again Alder," she cried.

"Shhh..." he comforted her, "It's okay...I know, old friend...I know..."

15

Siobhan and Casius walked the still-busy sidewalks of downtown Portland, making their way back to the alley that the werewolf recognized as a doorway to the dark grove. Siobhan was shocked that passersby rarely gave the odd-looking couple a second glance. But she had lived in Portland most of her adult life and the city was filled with the weird and wonderful. A werewolf and an elf would certainly not top out the weirdness scale and would be seen as cosplay.

"Why's Alder pissed at you?" Siobhan asked with no pretense.

"Oh, he's not...Saracin's exaggerating," her partner replied, averting the question.

"Deflection," Siobhan rolled her eyes. "Be straight with me wolf-boy."

She knew Casius almost as well as she did Derek. He cut his eyes in her direction and finally relented.

"Alright. Well, he's not exactly *upset* that I'm helping you look for Derek...he's more irritated at my motivation or what he *perceives* as my motivation," Casius replied.

"What does that mean?" Siobhan wrinkled her nose.

Stopping suddenly, he stared into the inky night sky for answers, "He thinks...he thinks I'm... in love with you."

"What!?" she cackled.

"It's crazy, right?" he chuckled with her.

As their laughter melted into the summer air, she was quiet momentarily before asking the obvious question, "You *aren't*, are you? I mean, that's awkward...and this conversation is going to take a different turn if you say yes."

"No! No, Von, I'm not in love with you," Casius clarified, shaking his head and continuing walking, "You just...remind me of someone...Someone we knew a long time ago. I enjoy that and your company. My brother's an asshole to think otherwise."

"So, *someone*, huh? Can I ask about *her*?" she quizzed.

"No...you may not," he chuckled again.

"Hmmm...we'll see," she teased.

Casius stopped cold, "Hey...we're here."

Peering down the narrow alley, he could feel the vibration of power hitting his chest. Closing his eyes, he felt for the center of the energy force as it would be that place where the door would be located. He took off, eyes still closed, down the dark alley, Siobhan close on his tail.

"Casius!" she whispered hoarsely. "Casuis!"

Freezing in place, he held out a palm, "It's here."

"Okay, so how do we get in?" Siobhan asked.

"Blood," he said flatly, pulled a knife from an ankle sheath, grasped it tightly, and drew it across his palm.

Thick crimson dripped on the ground. Reaching out, he touched the air with his palm and a violet light began to form a large person-sized rectangle around it that floated a foot off the concrete. With his palm still on the door, he pushed and it swung inside; the air around them filled with purple sparks and the stench of something like burning metal or rust.

He looked at Siobhan, "Hold on to my belt or my shirt and stay very close...don't let go or step off the path. This portal is alive. I've offered it the sacrifice, but I'm afraid if you don't stay with me, that glamour won't last long. We need to make sure it thinks we're one traveler...understand?"

Siobhan nodded, wrapping her arms around his waist, just to be sure.

"Just don't let go..." Casius repeated as they crossed the threshold together.

This portal was much different than the ones she had previously used. For the most part, they were generally creepy, and cold, and made you feel like you had cobwebs in your hair. The darkness in this one was more black than anything she had ever seen and the reddish-purple glow from the doors gave it an unsettling, eerie feeling; almost like they were being watched. Then there was the rhythmic vibration that was felt more than heard, like that of a heartbeat surrounding them on all sides.

Siobhan looked around her friend's broad chest to see him squeezing his bloody hand, leaving droplets on the path. It was only then that she noticed, in the creepy glow, that every inch of the passage was covered in sanguine fluid. They moved together slowly like a machine for several minutes until they reached the second door.

"This is going to be tricky," he warned. "I need you to jump on my back."

"What!?" Siobhan barked hoarsely.

"We stepped in together...that was easy. But getting out...all the weight needs to leave at once...so, time for a piggyback ride," he insisted.

Siobhan took a deep breath and jumped onto his back. Her legs barely reached around his broad chest as she hugged his neck. Casius again held out his hand, pushing hard, and jumped to the ground below; sparks scattered as the door slammed and went dark. Siobhan looked around to find them on a dirt path surrounded by trees.

Casius, wrapping his hand in a piece of cloth he tore from his shirt, leaned and whispered in her ear, "From here on out, you follow my lead, *Siae*."

Siobhan nodded.

They followed the path for about a mile when they saw, over the crest of a hill, a building with lights in the windows. As they got closer, it looked to be a somewhat derelict neighborhood long forgotten by possible war and time.

"Where are we?" Siobhan asked quietly.

Casius shook his head, "No idea yet."

The road widened a bit but was still very deserted as they continued to pass by one empty edifice after another. As they closed in on the only occupied building, they began hearing low, downtempo music playing. Lights showed in every window of the three-story industrial space and they noticed that a few people, mostly Elves, were hanging about in front. Casius and Siobhan climbed the seven steps to the front door confidently but kept their eyes low. A large elf, nearly as tall as Casuis put his hand on the werewolf's chest, stopping him.

"Who are you?" the elf growled.

Raising his head, Caisus's eyes met with the elves and a low growl emanated from his chest, "Remove your hand...or I'll have it for din-ner."

The elf never moved, "Go ahead...and I'll rip the heart from your chest and take your companion as my... *prize*."

The large elf and his friends laughed and then looked at Siobhan salaciously, licking his lips. With one swift movement, Casius grabbed the elf by the neck and lifted him off the ground, pinning him to the brick wall of the building. His friends moved forward on the attack, but Siobhan pulled the blade from its sheath on her back, guarding Casius. The group stopped their advance.

"Say again what your intent is on my friend?" Casius squeezed the elf's neck as his face turned magenta red. The elf struggled to shake his head.

One of his cronies took another step forward and Siobhan swung the curved blade, cutting a large lock of hair from above his ear.

"Next time, it's your head," she warned.

"Elf bitch!" he spat.

"Our friend here would like to apologize, isn't that right?" Casius snarled as the elf he still held by the neck did his best to nod before his eyes rolled to the back of his head, passing out. Casius let go of his throat and the elf dropped to the ground hard.

"Apology accepted," he said through grinding teeth as he stepped over the man. Siobhan, walking backward and keeping an eye on the rest, followed him inside.

Once in the door, the air was filled with music and clinking glasses. Not many turned their heads as Casius and Siobhan walked inside, but those that did kept their eyes down and looked away quickly. There was no decoration of any kind and the room was relatively sparse. A bar had been constructed in the middle of the large room with stools surrounding it entirely. There were few tables on the floor and the rest of the seating consisted of simple booths with mismatched wooden seating. The music was loud and they observed several people dancing in an empty space at the far side of the room.

The pair found an open table in the corner, sliding into its wooden booth seat. An older, plump Fae with short orange hair made her way over to them, setting two mugs of frothy ale on the table. Casius pulled out a small gold coin and flipped it at her. The woman grunted once, turned, and walked away.

Siobhan eyed him, "Interesting how you seem to be able to handle yourself in here. And why did you pay for these...we didn't order them."

"It's all they have...no need to order anything," he picked up his mug, taking a long pull.

"What are we doing here, Casius?" She wrapped her hand around the mug and pretended to drink.

"I'd say we probably need to be where we can get some information," he took another drink. "Trust me...they'll come to us. Just pay them no attention."

Siobhan took a drink from her mug and it tasted bitter on her tongue, but she swallowed it without wincing. She leaned into the conversation with Casius as the two spoke softly in the corner. Before long, a shorter, fat elf sauntered over and put his dirty boot on the seat next to Siobhan.

"Never seen you around here," his voice sounded like gravel as he spoke.

Siobhan cut her eyes at him, "Lucky me."

"Names' Orvym, you?" Orvym the elf introduced himself. Siobhan rolled her eyes as Casius laughed.

"I don't think my friend is interested, Orvym," Casius chuckled.

Orvym pursed his lips as he stroked a finger down Siobhan's arm, "I'm only looking for a dance."

Siobhan took a deep breath, "Touch me again, Orvym, and you'll be missing more than just that finger."

The portly elf looked down to see the barrel of Siobhan's gun pointed between his legs.

Orvym pulled his hand back slowly, "I'm...I'm not looking for any trouble...just lonely, that's all. Thought I'd show the new girl around...and...and her friend, of course."

He swallowed hard. Siobhan looked at Casius and he shrugged.

"Maybe you can help me," she grinned cunningly. "I'm Siae...this is my companion—"

Panic barreled over her as she didn't want to use Casius' real name, but they hadn't discussed what his cover would be.

Casius saved the moment, "Tyran...formerly of pack Crescent."

"Good to meet you. Are you two newly rogue?" Orvym asked, taking a large drink from his beer.

"No...we got snared by those damn tyrant Forehelien four winters back...helping a friend with some weaponry," Casius lied.

"Really? Who's your friend?" the elf asked.

Caisus finished his drink, "Doesn't matter...little human bastard killed her."

Orvym's eyes widened, "You don't mean...the Succubus?" He spat on the floor, "Forehelien scum."

"Right," Siobhan added.

"I heard that the piece of shit that killed her is Forehelien now," Orvym said.

"You don't say?" Sibohan faked interest, "Tyran and I are looking for a little payback...you wouldn't happen to know where the little shit can be found, would you?"

It made her sick to talk that way about Derek, but they needed information.

Orvym's beady eyes shifted between the pair, "I might know some-one...but..."

"But?" Siobhan asked.

"Information isn't cheap," The squat elf looked around the room. "I'm going to need something from you."

Casius and Siobhan gave each other a passing glance.

"What's your price, Elf?" growled Casius.

"Mmmm...we could start with a little dance with Orvym," he mused as he gazed at Siobhan.

Casius, growing impatient, spoke in a dangerously low tone, "I think the lady has already—"

"Fine," she cut him off, "I'm warning you Orvym, you so much as move your hands off my waist, I'll make you a head shorter."

Casius watched closely as Siobhan led the short elf to the small dance floor. The barmaid hobbled over to the table and sat another mug of ale in front of him. He gazed across the bar and prayed that the glamour Saracin concocted would hold.

16

—·—

Julia sat motionless on her wooden seat in the Conclave chamber as the speaker finished up what was most likely a very passionate commentary on the motivations of the most recent Changeling advance on the Fae. But, she couldn't be absolutely sure since she had really stopped listening more than a half hour before. In light of the recent disappearance of her son, the Order had called an emergency, late-night meeting to discuss the possible connections. Her mind and its own wandering thoughts betrayed her as she just couldn't focus on anything but Derek's whereabouts.

"In summation...we hold the truth that Varsa, former queen of the Montagne Blanche vampiric court should be held responsible for the uprising that has been wrought upon the realm and that should she be captured, she is turned over for judgment by our most honorable Queen. I now yield the floor to the Sovereign," a small Fae woman said in an airy voice; her large eyes shimmering like opals at Julia. "We hope that our pleas for swift action are taken seriously...that these dangerous interlopers meet swift justice."

Julia blinked, refocusing on the round table of onlookers, "Thank you, Lore, for your insight. Queen Vilotta of the Fae, you now have the floor."

"Thank you, Sovereign," she tapped her long, thin fingers impatiently. "While I appreciate the opinions of those of you gathered here, and applaud the support of my court, I am wondering when we can receive the troops to end this treacherous incursion?" Vilotta's voice was pitched higher than normal.

"You can't be serious." a gray-haired Elf said.

"You've got what we can give—" countered a female Vampire.

"Do you expect us to give you our children?" an older werewolf questioned harshly. The room devolved into a cacophony of rebuttals, arguments, and angry voices.

"Silence, please!" Julia bellowed, "Her Highness has the floor."

Vilotta continued, her pupils large, round, and hungry, "I am aware that we have many of the Brethren and Forehelien defending the Wilds, but surely we can pull from all resources as means of eradicating these...*enemies*. Why, there are several individuals still stationed here that we would welcome to join the defensive lines," She smirked. "All I ask is that we put right what was set asunder."

Vilotta returned to her seat at the table as the members of the Order quietly discussed and bickered among themselves.

"I believe King Novus of the Green Court now has the floor," Julia said, her voice growing weary.

An Elf sitting directly opposite her stood. He was of average height and exceptionally handsome, as was common, but especially so for one of his kind. He looked to be around the age of fifty, in human years, although his real age was deceptively older. His long, chocolate hair hung to his waist and was fitted with two braids at the temples that pulled away from his angular face. The silvery-green robes he wore hung to the floor and seemed to shift and glitter in the candlelight. He bowed his head slightly in Julia's direction before he spoke.

"Before I begin," his voice softly commanding, "I want to extend my court's condolences to her Sovereign at this time. Having been in the presence of your son, I can attest to his strength, fortitude, and honor. The Green Court stands by her Sovereign in this time of heartache."

Julia bowed her head, expressing her gratitude for his kind words.

"It is a difficult task...leadership. A task that each person around this table has had the courage, and privilege to undertake," Novus looked in the faces of each individual. "But what kind of leaders are we when we allow dishonorable and traitorous acts to go on under our very noses? We have lived in peace with one another for a long time. This peace has brought about advantages for all...are we not prosperous?"

He paused and watched several members nodding.

"It is unfortunate that we are but still infants in our ability to govern as leaders, together. Queen Vilotta, you speak as though we around this table have not given all we have to assist in your plight when the exact opposite is true. Our Brethren and Forehelien are working tirelessly to defend your home as if it were their own. But... we must also be pragmatic. We cannot leave any one place vulnerable because the timeline for success is not meeting your needs. This problem was not created overnight, nor will it be corrected overnight. You talk of eradication. My hope is that you are loose with your words and your desire is not the intentional destruction of the Changeling. Remember...they are signed members of our Treaty, by *your* hand, Queen. Let us all remember we have all lost someone precious to us in the war...some, more precious than others, and yet we continue on with the fight, together."

Novus, looking directly at Julia, lowered his eyes respectfully and bowed his head once more. Vilotta, enraged by his comments, threw herself from her chair.

"How dare you, King of the Green Court, to accuse me—"

King Novus shook his head, "Your Highness, I never intended to offend you. But, you forget why we are here...the disappearance of Derek Argent may well have happened as a result of your refusal to return to the peace table."

A soft murmur of agreeance made its way around the room.

"I will not offer asylum to those who have chosen revolution and then changed their minds! What is one *human* boy to the fate of thousands?" Vilotta charged, her pupils again thin, horizontal slits.

An audible gasp came from a few around the table.

"Vilotta, we are not talking about a mere human," Tobias Ne'De Sang's baritone voice rose over the crowd. "He *is* the Ascendant."

The Fae Queen's thin body trembled with anger, "Even more reason than to be rid of these vermin! I will not pander to scum!"

"Then you are sentencing your own people to war and death!" Lenias Grey growled. "Why should we continue to send in fighters for a war that will never end?"

Vilotta, maintaining her position at the table, stared into the golden globes of Lenias' eyes. Her voice becoming dangerously sharp, "It *will* end, you old hound! But your precious treaty makes this your problem as well."

Lenias raised his staff, slamming it to the floor again, "What you want, you crazy old sorceress, is genocide! You're just pissed off because some of your people finally stood up to you!"

The crowd murmured louder and the temperature of the room dropped thirty degrees. Vilotta's skin shimmered like crystal as her eyes bore down on the elder werewolf.

"Oh, piss off with your temper tantrum, Vilotta...the cold don't bother me," Lenias barked.

Tobias rose from his seat and with a swift movement put himself between the pair. He raised both hands at them, "Please, your Highness, Lenias...remember *where* you are."

Vilotta glared at Tobias, "Where is Dimitri? Hm? This entire meeting is a farce because members are missing. This is *his* fault! Had he dealt with that wife of his properly—"

She stopped short and Tobias looked down his nose at the Fae queen.

"Hmmm...if the vampire dealt with their own like they used to," her voice barely audible. Vilotta's skin returned to its normal paleness and the room became warmer as she backed away to her seat. Lenias' eyes watch her every move.

Julia gazed around the table at the faces of the members of the Order and remained in quiet contemplation. While she tried to keep her maternal feelings at bay, she couldn't help but feel hurt by Vilotta's disregard for her son. The Fae held very different beliefs regarding the relationships with their adult offspring and didn't view their life in any higher regard than anyone else, especially themselves.

Logically, Julia knew that Vilotta really didn't want to or even care to understand the idea of maternal love. She didn't care how Julia felt or have any empathy for the questions that filled her mind. If the rogue Changeling army had Derek, what would they want with him? Or worse, what would they *do* to him? A familiar, steady voice pulled her away from the darkening thoughts.

"Sovereign, what say you?" Tobias asked softly as all eyes lay on the graying woman.

"Queen Vilotta," she paused, "All remaining Brethren and Forehelien Charge will be made ready and will honorably serve to push back the Changelings that have disrupted the Wilds. But, it is now your turn to uphold the tenets of the Great Treaty and sit with those who desire a peaceful end to the fighting... Your allies will stand behind you in this task."

The Queen of the Fae glowered but never spoke.

"What of Lieutenant Argent, my lady?" Tobias urged.

She took a deep breath, "The search will continue for our Guardian of Portland Known. All information will be filtered through Alder Gray and Captain Vena." She paused looking directly into Vilotta's ravenous eyes. "They will remain here, at Arvendon."

17

—·—

Casius watched Orvym occasionally slide his hands down Siobhan's back in an attempt to grab her ass, only to have her position his hand appropriately and scold the short elf. He felt uncomfortable watching the struggle over and over but knew if he intervened, it would give the impression that she couldn't take care of herself.

Here in a dark grove, that could be her undoing. So, he sat and watched. When the music ended, Siobhan made her way back to their table corner with her dance partner following close like a puppy.

"Oh, Mistress Siae, thank you for a wonderful time. Can we do it again...soon?" he drooled.

Siobhan looked at him in disgust, "Orvym, you got what you wanted, now talk."

"But I..." his beady eyes blinked, "Can we have just one more?"

"Talk!" she ordered just as she felt a large hand on her shoulder. She spun around into the hairy, barreled chest of an enormous red-haired werewolf.

"Dance with me now!" his beer-laden breath demanded. He grabbed Siobhan around the waist, pulling her close.

"Get your hands off me!" she ordered, pulling away.

"Oh, come now, tart...show Ruct some love," he demanded as he manhandled her.

Casius struggled to get out of his seat as the larger werewolf continued to assault Siobhan. Orvym tried to intervene, but Ruct shoved the short elf into a nearby table of Fae. The Fae yelled and shouted insults at the elf and began beating on him as he cowered, covering his head. The beating drew the attention of a table of elves and they began throwing the Fae off Orvym which caused another chain reaction until the entire bar erupted in a full brawl.

Siobhan finally found her footing and threw a two-handed punch that made a direct hit in Ruct's chest and solar plexus. The werewolf stumbled back in time for Casius to catch him by his nape, throwing him into the back wall. Ruct was disoriented for a moment before he grabbed Casius by the arm, throwing him into a fresh pile of overturned tables. Siobhan drew her blade and swung at the towering werewolf, slashing his arm. The man howled in pain, whipping around to face off with Siobhan. His long arms, and dirty nails extended, swiped at her, tearing into the bare flesh of her arm. She yelled in pain, but steadied her sword, ready to take another pound of flesh.

Casius charged Ruct and drove him to the ground. The two men growled and wrestled as they tore at each other on the worn floor. Siobhan looked on trying to get a good position to strike their attacker but had no choice but to back away. After another moment, both men were standing again, exchanging punches when Siobhan rejoined the fight. Using a table for added height, she leaped into the air, completing a roundhouse kick to the back of Ruct's head. The werewolf turned to face her but when he did, Casius grabbed Ruct's head and chin, quickly snapping his neck. Ruct fell into a heap on the floor.

Siobhan stumbled over to Casius who was on one knee, panting. They surveyed the room to find the general destruction of broken furniture, glass, and bodies. Siobhan gasped as her eyes landed on Orvym. The squat elf lay not ten feet from where Ruct fell, himself broken and bloody. The pair slowly made their way to the dying man and leaned in as he tried to speak.

"Thanks for the dance, love," Orvym coughed blood.

"Hey! Orvym...you still haven't told me what you know," Siobhan did her best to comfort him, "I'm not letting you die...we had a deal."

He gagged on blood as he laughed, "Just like an Elf."

He closed his eyes.

"Orvym! Orvym!" Casius shook him. Like a miracle, his eyes popped open making Siobhan and Casius jump.

"Ziv..his...plan..." his eyes fluttered, coughing again. The blood made bubbles around his mouth as the elf closed his eyes a final time. Casius tilted his head, hearing a commotion in the near distance. He found a discarded bar rag and wrapped it around Siobhan's arm.

"We need to go! It's about to get real crowded here," he barked, grabbing Siobhan's hand. The pair ran through the back of the trashed bar, slipping out the back door as a group of vampires, smelling the fresh blood, rushed inside.

***

Casius held onto Siobhan's hand, dragging her through the wooded area behind the bar. They jogged for ten minutes cutting a chaotic path through the thickening forest. When he thought they had put enough distance between themselves and the building, he slowed them to a walking pace. Siobhan, who had run out of air several minutes prior, stopped to catch her breath.

"Hang...on...I need a minute," she panted, slumping at the waist with her hands on her hips.

Casius stopped to wait on her, "We need to go a little bit further...the more distance we put between ourselves and those vampires, the better."

"What are you talking about?" she asked as they started walking again.

"Rogue vampires...they smelled the blood and came running," he explained.

The pair spent the next thirty minutes in silence, making their way through the tangled vines and underbrush of the eerie woods. Casius led the way, pulling back large branches of overgrown trees so Siobhan could pass. When they came to the bank of a small stream, he took her on his back again, and jumped over, clearing the creek with little effort. When the werewolf finally felt at ease, they stopped to make camp for a few hours. Siobhan found a few dried logs and Casius started a fire as they settled in.

"How you doing over there?" he asked.

She grinned softly as she stared into the flames, "Holding up...you?"

"Hey, never better," Casius shrugged. "Thinking about Orvym back there...he said the name, Ziv, right?"

Siobhan's eyes moved over his, "Yeah, he did."

"Ziv...Ziv..." he muttered.

"Sounds like he's got a plan of some sort. You recognize him?" Siobhan asked.

"I don't know, maybe," he shook his head a little. He stood and came closer to Siobhan, checking her arm.

"Does it hurt?" he asked.

She nodded, "A little...I've had worse. I'm more worried about infection."

"I can take care of that," Casius began sniffing around their makeshift campsite.

"What are you doing?" chuckled Siobhan as she watched him walk around the perimeter smelling the air. The scene was comical and offered a bit of relief to the exhausted woman.

"Found it!" he jogged out into the darkness, pulled a plant out by its roots, and returned.

"What are you doing with that?" she asked as she watched Casius bite the heads off of a handful of flowers, petals and all, and chew them deliberately.

He motioned for her to raise her arm and still chewing, unwrapped the binding. He spat the mush of flowers and saliva into his hand and applied it to her wound then rebound it in the bar towel.

"Yarrow," he explained, "It's antibacterial...and should help stop the bleeding."

Siobhan's eyes widened, looking down at her arm, "Uhhh...thanks...boy scout."

"Those are the kids that dress in suits and spend the night in the woods, right?" Casius laughed.

She let out a loud chuckle, "Yeah...Casius...they are."

"I know things," his laughter became softer as he shrugged. "Alder and I used to scare them as cubs."

Siobhan burst into laughter, "You did not."

Casius shrugged and a pause fell between them.

"So," Siobhan sighed, "What now?"

"Now...we rest for a bit. We're gonna need to find this Ziv before daylight, I think. Then, get back through that doorway before you become *you* again," he replied.

"Ok," she nodded then whispered to herself. "Just hold on Reek...we're coming."

Casius leaned his back on a tree as several silent minutes passed between them, "Why do you call him that?"

Siobhan smiled to herself as she remembered a mud-caked and sweat-covered Derek as their team completed the Tough Old Mudder competition eight years ago. It was difficult. It was dirty. And it was the most fun she ever had.

"A group of us did this sort of race where you run and climb over obstacles," she chuckled, "Everything is dirt roads, water, and mud."

"Sounds like a good time," he smiled, closing his eyes.

"It was. But after...we were tired...and sweaty...and just filthy. He was so excited we finished that he jumped into a giant puddle and came out just covered...he thought we needed a big group hug...he stunk *so* bad," Siobhan's quiet tears trickled through her laughter.

Feeling her waves of heartache, Casius opened his eyes. He moved closer to her, putting his arm around her shaking shoulders.

"He...he smelled so bad...I called him 'Der-reek'...it just became our thing," she sniffed softly as her voice quaked.

Casius held her tightly as she quietly wept.

18

"Hey! Whoever you are...I'm thinking we can talk this out," Derek yelled into the darkness. His eyes had adjusted all they would in the dank cell and he could finally see the details of his cage. There were no windows and seemingly no outside walls. The cell appeared to have been constructed within another room with the only door being made of solid steel with a small barred opening. There were no furnishings, not even a bench. He was finally able to see the small red light just outside the door and knew it was a camera.

He rose from the floor and looked out of the bars, "I know you can hear me...what do you want?"

Silence.

"So...are you Changeling?" he asked.

No answer.

"Vampire?"

Silence.

"Succubus? They seem to hate me the most," he asked wryly. "The least you could do is tell me why I'm here," he yelled.

More silence.

He hit the door in frustration, "Damn it!"

Derek turned and sinking against the wall and his stomach growled. He wondered how long it had been since he was taken.

"So, what's your plan, huh?" he paused, "Not big on talking, I guess."

He heard a soft click.

"Where is she?"

"What?" Derek's heart dropped into his stomach as questions filled his mind.

"Where is she?" the voice of a male echoed off the empty room outside the cell.

"Who? Who are you talking about?" Derek asked, trying to maintain his calm. He rose to meet the voice at the small barred window. He couldn't make out anything in the darkness, not even a silhouette.

"Where is Ellie?!" the voice demanded angrily again.

Derek's temper became short, "Why don't you come in here and ask me face-to-face?"

"You will tell me where she is," the voice threatened.

"I have no idea who you're talking about!" Derek rushed door, pounding on it.

Wild laughter filled the air and he heard another *CLICK* as a door shut nearby. A few moments later, Derek could hear a hissing sound from just outside his cell door. The air smelled sweet like candy and he was becoming dizzy. He fought the drifting sense of unconsciousness as waves of lightheadedness crashed over him. Derek tried to hold onto himself and will the gas to shut off, but its effects had overtaken him. He couldn't speak or even form words as his heavy eyes closed and his body collapsed to the floor.

19

"**M**y lady, don't worry your mind with Vilotta...she will do what is right," Novus assured her. He closed the large wooden door behind the small group that made their way into her private office. Novus took a seat directly across from Julia's desk.

"She's acting like a child," Lenias Grey countered. "Stomping her feet when she doesn't get her way...par for the course with her."

"Regardless, we need to maintain a unified front and stand behind her. The Elven courts will continue to push her to find a peaceful end," Novus continued, "Imra sends her apologies that she could not make it tonight."

"The Fae have a difficult time dealing with situations that bring them boredom...Vilotta would rather end this as quickly as possible and move on," Julia stated softly.

"And wipe out an entire group to do it...its an extermination," Lenias growled.

Julia sighed, rubbing her temples, "Unfortunately, yes...My hope is that she remembers the Treaty before she acts rashly."

"Sovereign," the Elf king said gently, "What word have you received on your son?"

Julia shook her head and continued to rub her temples. The reality was that she hadn't heard anything since Alder informed her that

Casius and Siobhan were in Portland following up on leads. There had been no word from the Changeling resistance and no ransom demand from anyone. She was saddened that she was not given the opportunity to check in on Siobhan, as she had left in such a rush. She prayed to the universe that wherever they were, she and Casius were safe.

"Nothing," she replied. "No word from Alder...or Casius."

"Captain Vena tells me that the search is going around the clock," Novus confirmed.

"Julia, neither of my sons will leave a stone unturned," Lenias added and cleared his throat. "I noticed Dimitri missed another gathering...is everything alright?"

"He's been dealing with some things in his court. Varsa's betrayal made some waves he has needed to calm," she replied.

"Of course. And what of Silas? It's not normal that he hasn't been his father's stand in," he asked.

Julia shook her head. She hadn't seen Silas in a couple of days, not since the briefing. She was having a difficult time keeping up with her Forehelien.

"I can only imagine the Captain has him in the Wilds. We're using only a small handful searching for Derek," she sighed. "Keeping Vilotta appeased is more than a full-time job."

"Indeed," Novus nodded. "If there is anything I can assist with—" His voice trailed off as a firm knock rapped on the office door.

"Come!" Julia called.

The door opened to reveal Jaudon Grey, her hair pulled into a taught bun and her eyes seemed to glow with anticipation.

"Thank you Sovereign," she nodded, then acknowledged the other distinguished members in the room. "I have some news that might be of some interest."

"Please," Julia's voice begged.

"Father Grey," Jaudon smiled, giving the older man a kiss on the cheek before turning to the group. "I've met with my contact with the Portland police department. He assures me that they will get the word out about Derek. But as I was leaving, I got a call from Alder...turns out Casius and an unknown female elf were seen entering a dark portal."

"Oh the Gods!" gasped Julia.

Lenias' face turned red, "What in the hell does that son of mine think he's doing, and with who!?"

Julia's voice rose with panic, "Lenias, I've got a bad feeling about this." She took a deep shaking breath, "Casius would never leave Siobhan alone...especially now...I just wonder if—"

"If they've gone and done something stupid?" Lenias barked.

Julia nodded.

"My son will never hear the end of this!" he growled. They both stared at each other in disbelief as Jaudon softly broke the tension.

"I think we all need to relax...we know for a fact that she isn't typical for a human. She's tough...and just as well trained as any Forehelien. What I think is worth noting is that a dark portal was found not six blocks from Derek's studio and could have easily been used as an escape route for whoever took him."

Julia nodded, "I have to have faith that they will be alright. And you're right, that is definitely noteworthy...but..."

Lenias studied Julia, "I know that look...you're gut is telling you something."

"What is it, Julia?" Novus asked.

Her eyes bounced between the three in front of her, "I don't know...something is...off...about the entire situation. It doesn't feel right."

"How so?' Jaudon pressed.

Julia shook her head, making her way back to the chair behind her desk, "Up until Derek's disappearance, the Changelings have never attacked anything outside the Wilds...not once. Even though they know Vilotta has the whole of the Hidden armies behind her. They stay focused in that territory."

"Their fight is certainly directed...it's clearly against Vilotta," Novus offered.

"Yes," she replied emphatically.

"So, you're wondering why they suddenly chose to move against Arvendon," Jaudon stated as Julia nodded again.

They were still for a moment in pregnant silence. The Changelings war was never with Arvendon, the Order, or the Treaty, but about Vilotta's treatment of them. So why would they all of a sudden change their focus and move against the seat of the Hidden? The kidnapping of the Ascendant was obviously a bold, offensive play; but it did not seem logical. There had to be more to Derek's disappearance.

"That's a very good question," Lenias wondered aloud, "A very good question indeed."

20

S ilas opened the closet and stepped out of the portal. He found the small office at Arvendon empty as usual, making his way to the room's door to check the hallway. Just as he stuck his head out, he heard someone clear their throat behind him.

"Councilor Montagne Blanche," the ethereal voice said.

Silas spun to find Lore sitting in the corner of the room. He looked around suspiciously before addressing her.

"Where did you come from?" he demanded hoarsely.

Lore's large, opal eyes glittered, "I am Fae."

"Yes, I know," he replied, raising an eyebrow.

"We are eternal and constant," she grinned.

"That doesn't answer my question," Silas said flatly.

"Doesn't it?" Lore tilted her head.

Closing his eyes, Silas sighed, "Nevermind. What do you want? Shouldn't you be following your queen around?"

"Yes. But my conversation with you is more important at the present time," she folded her hands in front of her. "Silas of Montagne Blanche, we need to talk as they say."

"About?"

"The location of your mother, Varsa," she replied airily.

"Like I told Vilotta, I don't know—" Silas said before being cut off.

"Do you know what I am, Silas?" Lore asked.

Rolling his eyes, he huffed, "Fae."

"Of course. But what I really am?" she asked again.

Silas shrugged.

"I am the Librarian. Which, for Fae is very rare...even more rare than your friend, the Kiada," Lore explained.

"Okay."

"I record every detail of Fae existence. I have all the knowledge of the Fae right here," she pointed a pale, thin finger to her temple. "I also study the other races of the Hidden. I've studied you and your kind since before time...which is how I know you are lying."

Silas cleared his mind of all thoughts of his father and Varsa. He didn't know if Fae could feel heartbeats or smell pheromones, so he did his best to control that too.

Lore smiled at him, "I'm not reading your mind, Silas. But I know you and your father are keeping Varsa at his chateau. Probably because Dimitri thinks it's safer for everyone involved. It was a good plan."

No matter how hard he tried to keep his facial expressions to a minimum, Silas could not help but be in shock. There was no way for her to know all of the details. He was certain he had been careful with every word that he said to anyone over the past year. However, part of him did feel a bit of relief.

"There's no need to admit to me that I'm right...because I already know. But, I do have a proposition for you," Lore continued.

"I'm listening," he replied with caution.

"Queen Vilotta is dangerously close to crossing a line that could crumble the reality of Fae. I would like your help keeping her within bounds," she explained.

"I'm going to need a little more than that," Silas snickered.

"A Fae's word is their bond...and it is unbreakable. Your kind speak to one another in a common language and never consider the true consequence of the meaning of your words. Fae are their words. Those words are vows. We hold honor in that. When a Fae breaks their words...their vows...their bond...it is as egregious as death. There is no worse evil," she said.

Silas was trying hard to wrap his mind around what she was saying, "And Vilotta is close to breaking a vow?"

"Yes," Lore stated as a matter of fact, the inflection of her voice never wavering.

"What vow?" he asked.

Lore opened her mouth to speak, but the voice that came out was Vilotta's.

" *'Insolent little...pests! I'll have them all bound and begging for the sweet release of death...Even more reason than to be rid of these vermin! I will not pander to scum!'*"

"*Merde*!" Silas took a step back from the Librarian, "That's unsettling."

"I am the repository for all Fae knowledge," she said in her own voice.

"Right..." he eyed her closely, "But I still don't understand. You say she's on the verge of...breaking a vow? How?"

"When Vilotta became queen, she swore an oath to be a leader and protector of *all* Fae...if she were to act now upon her words," Lore responded, her voice otherworldly.

"She would be breaking her oath to her people...got it," Silas nodded. "Why don't you confront her...since you're the keeper of the knowledge."

Lore was unsettlingly quiet for several minutes before speaking again.

"Do you know how Fae receive their Queens?" she asked, and Silas shook his head. "A Fae queen is only ever replaced when she no longer holds true to her word. At that time, she faces a challenger in a battle of conference...it is a battle to the death. If the challenger wins, they assume the role of queen; if the sitting queen wins... well, they keep their position and reputation. Vilotta is our third Queen."

Narrowing his eyes on Lore, Silas grew impatient, "So, why don't you challenge her? Surely having all the knowledge of the Fae would be an advantage."

Shaking her head, Lore replied, "I am no challenger...I am the Librarian."

"And...so?" he pushed.

"I am the Librarian. I serve the Fae," she reiterated strongly. "Which is why I need your assistance, Silas of Montagne Blanche. You will help me serve the Fae honorably."

"How's that?" the hair on the back of his neck bristled. He knew that making a deal with the Fae could not just be disastrous, but potentially deadly.

"You will assist with the relocation of refugees from the Wilds and, in return, I will not reveal the location of your mother," she proposed.

"What refugees?" Silas demanded.

"Not all of the Changelings are fighting in this war. Some strongly oppose what is taking place. But Vilotta refuses to see the difference. Then there are the Fae that are being hurt because they are caught in the crossfire. I want to get anyone who wants out to a safe location...until this can be resolved properly," she explained.

Silas considered her proposition. He knew it would be energy wasted denying to her Varsa's location; she had him dead to rights. And he suspected she may be able to tell if he was lying although he didn't know how. In a way, he understood the Fae. *His* word was his honor also and he made an oath a very long time ago to protect the inhabitants of the Hidden, at all costs. A deal with the Fae always came with a very steep, often undisclosed price though. He weighed his options carefully. He could either enter into an agreement with Lore the Librarian of the Fae and risk a double cross or he could refuse. If he did, he would be putting his father's rule and the Great Treaty in jeopardy.

"What do you need me to do?" he asked with conviction.

Lore nodded, raised her palm to him, and glided closer, "So I have your bond, vampire?"

Raising his palm, Silas placed his hand on hers, "You do."

"As it will be," Lore smiled. You will assist with the evacuation of displaced and loyal Fae from the Wilds and I will not call for your mother's release to Queen Vilotta."

Lore withdrew her hand from Silas's and placed it on his face. Her thin fingers cradled his strong jaw as she pulled him in for a kiss.

A small wave of energy, not unlike static electricity moved through Silas's body. The conductivity was not unpleasant and he thought it felt quite nice. As he pulled away, he realized her lips tasted like strawberries.

'Fae magic,' he thought.

"We will need somewhere large to house all who choose to leave. Can you find a place?" Lore's opal eyes glittered in the light.

Silas nodded, "Yeah... I think I have an idea."

21

Casius and Siobhan rested for a couple of hours, deciding to make their way to the next town in search of the mysterious Ziv. After leaving the cover of the forested area, they found a narrow, overgrown road that led them north. The sky was crystal clear overhead and the waxing moon elongated the shadows of the trees away from them. Siobhan took in her surroundings and it occurred to her that she didn't know where she was.

"Do you know where we are, exactly?" she asked.

Casius frowned, looking around, "You mean other than the dark grove?"

"Yeah."

"This feels like Russia," he replied.

"Russia?!" Siobhan exclaimed.

"Looks like Russia...smells like Russia," Casius shrugged.

Siobhan chuckled, "You say that like we got here like normal people."

"Oh, well..." he glanced at her, "Yeah, I see your point."

Silence fell between them as they walked.

"I don't think I'm ever going to get used to all of this," she sighed.

"What do you mean, all of this?" he asked.

"I mean," Siobhan thought for a moment, "I literally can open a door in my house, walk a few steps and I'm eight hundred miles away. You can read minds. I live with a baby that burps fire. Sometimes—"

"Sometimes it's a lot," Casius finished for her.

"It is."

"Do you regret it?" he eyed her.

Siobhan was quiet for a long moment, thinking about his question. Did she regret the last few years? The friends she made...the family that accepted her? Did she regret falling in love with Derek? That last thought made her physically ill. Even imagining a life without him made her stomach churn; she could not and *would not* envision it.

Siobhan shook her head emphatically, "No...not at all."

Casius nodded; he knew she meant what she said. They walked a little further, always keeping an eye on the tree line. Casius focused his hearing as far as it would go, but as far as he could tell, there wasn't another person around for miles.

"So, tell me about this woman I remind you of," Siobhan smiled.

He cut his eyes at her but stayed silent.

"Oh, c'mon Casius...tell me. How fair is it that you know so much about me and I know nothing about this person?" she pushed.

"That argument made no sense," he chortled.

"Yeah...well, I'll use lack of decent sleep as my excuse," Siobhan grinned. "Spill it."

Casius sighed heavily, "Alright...if it'll get you off my back."

"Not likely."

"Fine," he rolled his eyes. "Her name was Rani. We had been together and trained together as cubs....even born on the same day...a year apart. She was a warrior in every sense of the word. We joined the Brethren together and planned to join the Forehelien together."

"But you didn't?" Siobhan said softly.

Casius' stone gray eyes looked pained as he remembered, "No...we...we never got the chance."

Siobhan wanted to know the rest of the story but felt awful for asking. It dawned on her, however, that Rani seemed to mean more to Casius than just a friend or someone he served with over the years. Siobhan had questions in her mind but her heart was too broken *for* him to ask them. After a long moment, she finally thought of the right words.

"You loved her, didn't you?" she asked gently.

Casius swallowed hard, "I did...I...I still do."

"How did it happen?" Siobhan coaxed.

"We got some bad intel on a rogue hideout. This job...it's always dangerous work...we were there to capture a werewolf couple that had attempted an assassination on one of our elders. Everyone was armed with silver bullets."

He hung his head.

"Rani checked the corner but as she moved around it, she took a bullet to her neck. It was... friendly fire," his voice barely audible.

"Oh my God," Siobhan whispered. "I'm so sorry."

Casius' face became peaceful, "Thanks. It *was* an accident...nothing more. She was something special though...you remind me a lot of her."

"Casius.."

He chuckled, shaking his head, "Not like that. Rani...was my little sister and my best friend."

Siobhan allowed the revelation to wash over her. She had no idea there were once three Grey Pack children, she had always assumed it was only Alder and Casius. She instantly recognized the pain Casius felt at the loss because she knew that pain all too well. Death was never something a person got used to seeing or reliving, but the utter hole it created in a sibling suddenly left behind was immeasurable.

"She was strong–willed, fierce...damn good in a fight. She was fear-less too. But she also had this light about her. She was beautiful...but she didn't seem to know it. She had men falling over themselves. That was pretty annoying, actually," he laughed. "And she just *got* me, you know?"

Siobhan reflected on his words before she spoke again.

"I do. And...that's why Alder thinks you're in love with me," she said.

He raised an eyebrow, but let her continue.

"He sees how close we are...You aren't attached to anyone...he sees it as infatuation."

"But, I'm not—" he interrupted.

"I know that...but he doesn't. He's only seeing from the objective of an observer. He doesn't have your abilities, Casius. He can't read your mind all the time," Siobhan explained. "I'm sure he knows you've grieved your sister...but he doesn't know if you moved past it."

"I don't even know if I have," Casius commented.

She smiled at him, "Yes, you have...you still love her, you always will...but you *have* moved on. Otherwise, our relationship would be so much different than it is."

She stopped walking to face him, "Casius...you and I...we're family, we both know it's always been that way."

The werewolf smiled broadly at her; he knew she was right. Next to Alder, Siobhan was probably the closest thing he had to a sibling. That realization made him feel complete and like a missing piece of his heart had finally locked in place.

He smiled at her once more, "Yeah, you are kinda like a little sister."

Siobhan looked distressed for a quick moment and it wasn't lost on Casius.

"Oh, Von...I'm sorry...I didn't—" he apologized.

She shook her head, "No...don't apologize...that's a great description...and I'm honored. Besides, I've realized I can't change the past...no matter how hard I want to."

Casius wrapped his arm around her, hugging his friend, "We just accept it and keep moving."

He released his hold, stopping in the middle of the road, "Speaking of moving...we've got someone headed our way, here...let's get in the tree line."

The pair rushed to make themselves hidden among the high bushes and pines then waited quietly. A few minutes passed before Siobhan could hear the pounding of quick feet on the road. They looked through the cover to see a dark-haired elf weaving as he ran. Siobhan could barely see him from where she crouched, but she thought he looked injured. In the near distance, the sounds of shouting could be heard.

Casius narrowed his eyes, staring at the man on the road, "Son of a..."

To Siobhan's surprise, Casius bolted from their hiding spot and ran to the man as he stood, bent over, panting. Casius grabbed the elf by his uninjured arm, pulling him into the low ditch where he himself had been hidden just moments before.

He whispered hoarsely at Siobhan, "Keep him quiet...stay here."

Casius ran back into the road and waited. Just seconds later, an exceptionally tall elf slowed her jog, cautiously approaching him. From what Siobhan could see, she carried a long bow in her right hand and a tattered quiver on her back. She looked a little gaunt now, but Siobhan could see the elf was once quite beautiful.

"Oi! You! Who are you?" the elf called to Casius.

He raised his eyebrow, "Since you're the one in a hurry, you first."

With the swiftness of lightning, she drew her arrow down on Casius.

"I asked you a question...mut," she snarled.

Casius put his hands in the air, "Meant no offense...I'm Tyran."

"Tyran. I've heard of you. You see a slimy piece of rat shit scurry through here? He'd probably be bleeding...I nicked him, I'm sure of it," she replied.

"No," Casius lied, "But I did pick up a scent of blood about two klicks that way."

He pointed south.

"Hmmm...slippery little bugger. Guess I better find him before the vampires do," she said backing away slowly with the sliver point of the arrow still targeted on Casius' chest. "Now, be a good boy and stay right there."

The dark-headed elf lying next to Siobhan began to move and Casius started growling to cover his movement in the brush. Siobhan cupped her hand over the elf's mouth, shaking her head fiercely as the man finally came around.

"Now... let's be friends mut..." the elf said as she turned on her heel, disappearing into the western forest. Casius stood quietly for another moment and listened to her footsteps fading away from them. When he was confident she bought his ruse, he turned quickly and ran into the underbrush.

Grabbing the man under the uninjured shoulder, Casius whispered again, "C'mon...we need to get out of here."

"What's going on?" Siobhan asked as she helped steady him.

"I'll explain in a minute," Casius said as they raced through the trees. "If you see any of that plant I used last night, grab it along the way."

While they struggled to keep a good pace, Siobhan and Casius finally made it with their burden to an open clearing at the edge of the wooded area. It looked as though this was yet another abandoned town that had found its demise years prior to the ravages of war. It was a much smaller settlement than the one from the night before, but no less dangerous. The trio stayed at the edge of the forest and waited to go unnoticed before making a run to a small empty shed.

Siobhan pried back the rusted tin of the structure just allowing Casius' large body to squeeze through. He then dragged the elf in behind him and Siobhan followed. The space was small and a section of the roof had rotted, falling in a few years ago. It was mostly empty except for two old bales of hay and a single shelf still standing in a back corner. Casius propped the elf upright against the old hay.

Ripping open the man's shirt he opened his palm in Siobhan's direction. Reaching into the small back pocket of her pants, she pulled out a smashed bundle of the yarrow. Casius repeated the same process from the night prior and filled the shoulder wound with the green poultice then tied a strip of the man's shirt around as a bandage. The elf had fully woken when Casius sat him down and watched the werewolf as he worked.

"That should do it," Casius said to the elf.

Siobhan looked between the two men, "Do what? What's going on?"

"I just got us some backup...and maybe intel," Casius commented as he sat himself across from the elf. "But first, I'd like to know what you did to get yourself shot...*again*... Vaegril."

A large smirk spread across Vaegril's very handsome face.

22

— · —

The pounding on the door was relentless, driving Theo hurriedly down the wooden staircase.

"Goddamn, it! If whoever this is wakes her up...I swear," he muttered under his breath. He could see the silhouettes of two figures through the stained glass of the Victorian door as he reached for the knob. As he released the locks, the knocking ceased and he pulled the door open.

"Can I help you?" he asked, putting his finger to his lips as he spoke softly, closing the door behind him.

The two men were professional-looking, both dressed in black slacks. The man on the right wore a light blue golf-style polo while the man on the left wore a salmon pink button-up with a grey and blue paisley-designed tie. They held badges out to Theo that identified them as detectives with the Portland Police Department. Theo immediately felt underdressed as he stood barefoot, shirtless, in only his dark blue cargo-style shorts.

"Sorry," he apologized, "My daughter is sleeping."

The man on the right, Jack Rollings, smiled, "Oh yeah, how old?"

"Four months," Theo beamed proudly.

"Ahh, that's great man, congratulations! I've got two at home...twins, six months," the detective replied. "We're sorry to call so early...but we're looking for Siobhan Miles. Is she home?"

Theo frowned, shaking his head, "No...is this about Derek?"

"Would this be Derek Argent?" Sergeant Rollings asked.

"Yeah...he disappeared the night before last. He and Von are supposed to get married today," Theo replied.

"We've been trying to get a hold of Ms. Miles for a few days. We have something of a sensitive nature to discuss with her. But our department has been in contact with Jaudon Grey regarding the disappearance of Mr. Argent, is that still a good contact?" the man on the right asked.

"Yeah...yeah, of course," Theo said. "What's this about?"

Rollings handed Theo a thick business card, "If you talk to her or if Ms. Miles comes home, please have her give me a call at this number."

He took the card and nodded, "Absolutely."

The men nodded their thanks. They turned to leave and Theo shut the door behind them. He leaned on the frame, thinking for a long moment. Shoving the card into his pocket he ran up the stairs to grab his phone. There was only one thing that he could think of that would put the Portland Police Department on their doorstep.

23

Derek's head swam as he tried to focus on the burgeoning commotion around him. The bright light hitting his face was blinding as he struggled to open his eyes. The man in front of him was blurry and moved slowly like he was walking through Jell-O. Derek worked against his own body to force his eyes from closing but it seemed they had a mind of their own. The fog in his head became thick and he fought the urge to vomit.

Suddenly, a white hot fire burned in his chest and Derek cried out in pain.

"Son of a bitch!" his eyes flew open in an attempt to concentrate on the blurry figure of the man.

"I asked you a question...where is she!" the man yelled.

Derek shook his head, "I don't...I don't know—"

"Devil! I won't believe your lies! Where is she?!" the voice boomed again in his face.

Derek tried to headbutt the figure in front of him, but his body felt too heavy. He then felt fire pierce the skin on his chest once more.

He howled in pain as it seared through him, "I don't know who she is! You've got the wrong guy!"

The adrenaline began to pump through his body making Derek feel more alert. He opened his eyes once more and the man in front of him came into focus. He held a simple five-inch hunting knife in one hand and a kitchen blowtorch in the other. Derek watched as the balding man heated the knife until it glowed red. The man dropped the blowtorch on a short table next to him and held the blade tip at Derek's throat.

"You will tell me what I want to know," the man growled, "Because God commands it, devil."

The man drug the hot knife down Derek's bare chest and the world went dark once more.

24

— · —

"Vaegril? Do you know him?" Siobhan asked as she stared at the elf.

He was tall, nearly the same height as Derek, and his thin frame carried with it lean muscle. He was naturally attractive but looked like he was in need of some new clothing as his were dirty and tattered. Vaegril's eyes were the most unusual as they seemed to pierce through someone with deadly efficiency. A fleeting thought of recognition hit her as she stared at the sharpness of the crystal peridot orbs, but couldn't remember from where or when.

Casius chuckled, "I should. We've served together in the charge for the last twenty years."

"Casius...you're a sight for sore eyes," Vaegril coughed a short laugh, shaking the werewolf's hand. "What are you doing here?"

"Looking for someone...Julia's son is missing," he replied.

Vaegril's eyes widened as he looked from Casius to Siobhan, "No shit? Damn. Who took him? And...who's this?"

He raised his chin toward Siobhan.

"This is his fiance. Siobhan, meet Vaegril of the Green Court," Casius introduced the pair.

"No way...I heard he's marrying a common human. Whoever this is...is lying to you, Casius," Vaegril disagreed firmly. But before the elf could drop his eyes, Siobhan had

unsheathed Liarshank, cupping it under his chin. The sword began to vibrate with energy.

Vaegril swallowed hard, staring at the blade, "I have to ask love, where did you get that fine piece of armory?"

Siobhan gripped the hilt tighter and as she did, the sword seemed to lighten, as if it knew how to make itself more comfortable in her hand. She even thought she felt it lurch toward the man. Siobhan stared at the elf, watching him become more nervous as the seconds ticked by.

"Look...I know you don't like me...but," he swallowed again, still staring at the glittering blade. "We can be friends, just this once."

Siobhan cut her eyes in confusion in Casius' direction. To her surprise, he looked amused at the elf's trepidation. "Is he talking to the sword?"

"Casius! Whoever she is, make her put it down...please!" Vaegril begged, now visibly sweating.

"She doesn't like to be called *human*...and trust me...she's far from common," Casius guffawed.

Vaegril deftly jumped to his feet, just missing the tip with his chin, and placed his face uncomfortably close to Siobhan's as she lowered the still-vibrating blade. He eyed her closely, his eyes peering at every detail of her features. Suddenly, he began to laugh wildly.

"Holy. Shit. That's a spectacular veil...that's Saracin's work...and her blade," he gave a low whistle. "She just keeps getting better. How is Sari, by the way."

He continued to eye Siobhan.

"Still hates you," Casius shrugged.

"Yeah...that scar still twinges a bit," the elf replied as he lifted his shirt to show Siobhan a thick, white raised area right above his pubic bone.

"Saracin did that?" she asked. "Why?"

"I ask myself the same thing," he mused.

The blade quivered harder in her hand.

"Couldn't be that she was pissed off at you for the way you dumped her sister," Casius replied.

Vaegril looked dramatically devastated, "I dump her? No sir...she was clearly the dump-er, I the innocent dump-ee."

"You've never had an innocent moment in your entire life, elf," Casius roared with laughter.

"Not true! And Miria broke my heart," his voice whined like a child.

Casius rolled his eyes, "You left her a note...then drowned your sorrows in that trainee from the Blue, V."

Vaegril shrugged, "Well...she did say we should see other people."

Siobhan finally sheathed Liarshank and Vaegril backed away. He smiled provocatively at her and pointed.

"It suits you...you're gorgeous," he winked.

Casius sighed in exasperation, "Alright, Romeo...she's spoken for. But we could use your help."

"I never could say no to a beautiful woman," the elf replied, "And...after all you did save me from what would, I'm sure, have been a painful death at the hands of Sillia. What'dya need?"

"Intel...we're looking for someone named Ziv...heard of them?" Casius asked.

Vaegril raised his eyebrows nodding, "Yeah...but I heard he left the grove several weeks ago."

"To where?" Siobhan demanded.

"One would assume somewhere near you, my dear," Vaegril's familiar eyes sparkled.

Casius frowned, "Why? Why near Siobhan?"

The elf's eyes darted between the pair, "Because his mate is being held at Arvendon...you didn't know that?"

"Who's his mate?" Casius and Siobhan asked simultaneously.

Vaegril chuckled, "You really do need my help...Ziv is Incubae..."

"Asha," Siobhan whispered. The elf winked again, confirming her identity to the pair.

"Wait," Casius paused, "Zivhala? That's who we're talking about? We thought he was dead."

Siobhan turned to Casius, "They went after Derek!"

"Von, we don't know that for sure...and Asha is secure in the prison. No attempts at an escape," he replied.

"Prisoner exchange?" Vaegril suggested.

Casius thought for a moment, "Not that we're aware of...but—"

"But?" the elf asked.

"But we've been here since last night...eight hours, maybe? There could've been a demand made," Casius offered.

"Casius, we need to get back to Portland," Siobhan's voice shook.

He nodded, "V, where is the closest portal?"

"Oh man...back south...the same general direction you send Sillia," Vaegril replied.

"Well, we've got no choice...you with us?" Casius asked.

A devious grin spread across the elf's face, "Hell yeah...it's time I moved on to the next grove anyway."

A rustle could be heard just outside the neglected barn and Casius raised a finger to his mouth, gesturing to the pair to be quiet, then pointed to the far corner. Vaegril's eyes darted in the same direction as Siobhan pulled Liarshank from her sheath. The trio quietly began backing their way out when something grabbed Siobhan's foot from under a side door.

"Son of a bitch!" she yelled and immediately the barn doors were torn from what remained of their hinges as they were surrounded by four vampires.

"Well, well, well...what do we have here?" A tall, lanky vampire with greasy, jet-black hair sneered. Two elves and a hound." He slinked his way toward Siobhan as the others laughed. "Well, aren't you a pretty little thing."

Liarshank vibrated in Siobhan's hand as the man drew closer.

"What do you want?" Casius barked. The group's leader spun on his heel to face the werewolf.

"Us?" he eyed his group, "Oh, we're just weary travelers lookin' for someplace to get some rest...and a snack."

His comments elicited another round of snickers from his small band.

Siobhan looked at each vampire, noticing they looked ill and gaunt. Their pale skin seemed to cling to their bones as the muscles underneath appeared sinewy. Their overall presence was made even more intimidating by the look of their coal-black eyes. She knew they weren't just hungry; they were ravenous. At the same time, however, she'd never seen a vampire look so diseased.

"Look, we're just passing through...no need to make a bad situation worse here," Vaegril smiled with transparent diplomacy.

"What a coincidence...so are we." Within seconds, the leader was at Siobhan's side with his pale hand around her throat, "Boys...I say we start with dessert first. Sweetheart...kindly drop your blade."

Siobhan never flinched, but she tightened her grip on the hilt of the sword. Casius caught her eye and made a slight shake of his head at her.

He knew they would have to fight their way out, but he didn't want Siobhan to get hurt in the process.

"I wouldn't do that if I were you," Casius laughed wildly.

The leader licked his lips with near insatiable hunger, "Whys that wolf?"

Casius took a small step forward, forcing the two vampires that flanked him to move within reach.

"She'll probably take it personally," he shrugged.

As he finished his sentence, he dug his hands into the necks of the two vampires, ripping out their tracheas. Thick blood spattered the walls, pouring onto the ground before their lifeless bodies had time to hit the floor. Vaegril, anticipating his former partner's move, dropped to the ground, pulling a small silver stake from a makeshift ankle holster. He sprung from the ground and drove the metal spike through the center of vampire number three's skull. Both men turned just in time to watch Siobhan spin in place, raise Liarshank, and completely slice the leader in half at the waist. His body fell on either side of her in two pieces.

The three of them stood for a moment, taking in the carnage that surrounded them. Casius made his way over the dead to get to Siobhan. He could feel her shaking before he reached out to touch her shoulder. As he did, she startled, whipping the sword in his direction, just missing his throat.

"Whoa there!" Vaegril cried, running toward the pair.

Casius held up his hands, "Von? You okay?"

She stood panting with quiet fear for a few more moments before slowly sliding the wet blade back into its leather sheath on her back. Siobhan swallowed hard, "I'm fine. Why...why do they look like that!?"

"They're starving," Vaegril explained. "Vampires' natural food source is human blood...can't get that here...the only thing they can find is elven."

Siobhan, still breathing hard, looked confused, "What about werewolf blood?"

"Poison," Casius raised an eyebrow. "A little evolutionary protection my people developed over thousands of years. They can drink it...but it'll make them sick."

She continued to look around at the scene. Caisus could feel her relaxation as the adrenaline in her body began to subside. He knew he needed to get her out of the grove, now more than ever. If the vampire had been able to actually bite her, their ruse would've been over.

"What do we do now?" she asked calmly.

"We get the hell out of here," Vaegril ordered. "It won't be long until more vampires show up."

"I want to know about Ziv," Siobhan demanded angrily.

"Sure sweetheart...we can talk about him. After we get some distance between us and..." he motioned to the bodies.

"Von, c'mon...let's go," Casius urged.

She finally nodded and the trio made their way back the way they came, heading into the eastern woods. They all agreed it was much too dangerous to take the road that would lead them directly back to the dark portal, so they cut their own way through the forest. Vaegril's wounded arm made the journey that much more difficult as they were forced to walk, not run, most of the way. Hiking for around thirty minutes, Siobhan couldn't take the silence any longer. She was near bursting with anxiety and wanted to know what Vaegril knew. She stopped in the middle of the path to catch her breath.

"Alright...we're far enough away. Tell me about Ziv," she ordered.

Vaegril turned to face her as Casius took a seat on a nearby boulder.

"What do you want to know?" the elf winced as he rubbed his arm.

"Who is he? What does he look like? How is he going to help Asha escape? Whatever you got," she replied.

The elf nodded, taking a deep breath.

"Ziv and Asha were loyal followers of Daria...acolytes if you will. Asha was always Daria's right hand...which, only bolstered Daria's position, in my opinion," Vaegril explained.

"Why?" Casius asked.

He raised his eyebrows, "You how they are...for a Succubae, the only 'I' in team is 'me'...but for some reason, Ziv and Asha believed in Daria's little plans. Once they started following her, it didn't take long for more to join. Then she got herself killed. Thanks for that by the way."

He winked at Siobhan, continuing, "Then Varsa took over...her *rule the world* view was a little more bloody but...it still seemed to fit the master plan. Now that she's out of the picture...Ziv is looking to put Asha on the throne."

"But like Casius said...she's in prison. How does he think he's going to do that?" Siobhan asked.

"Succubae are...slick...smart. My guess? He's got a grift going already, but it isn't money he's after this time...it's power," Vaegril proposed.

"What does he like now?" Casius wondered.

"No idea," he shrugged. "I do know that he didn't fit in here...at this grove."

"What do you mean?" Siobhan pressed.

Vaeril shrugged, "Look around...this is a pretty hard place...and not what you would call cosmopolitan. Ziv likes nice things: suits, wine, cars...*none* of the luxuries found here."

Casius eyed Siobhan as the revelation that they were indeed in the wrong place poured over them. He felt her anxiety and the relentless grip of desperation building that he knew was linked to her desire to get through the portal.

"Okay," he relented, "Let's go home."

They set off through the woods once more in silence. Siobhan's mind began to wander as she hiked. What if they were too late? What if a ransom offer had been made and Derek was already home...or dead? She shook her head. She couldn't think about the worst-case scenario right now, she needed to focus on the task at hand. Getting back to the portal and going home. She started thinking about matters closer to her at the moment. She wondered why the female elf, Sillia shot Vaegril in the first place. As if Vaegril could read her mind, the elf broke the silence himself.

"You're wondering why she shot me," he commented.

"I'm not," Casius snarked as a smile crossed his face.

"I was curious," Siobhan admitted but shocked that he so accurately knew what she was thinking.

Vaegril shrugged, "I did something I probably shouldn't have...she got upset. Sillia always had a tendency to overreact."

She eyed him suspiciously.

"I bet," she muttered.

"No, really...she's a very...*passionate* woman," he insisted.

"Oh God," Casius mumbled as he walked a bit ahead.

"I'm also quite passionate...I may have gotten carried away and hurt poor Sillia's feelings," the elf bragged.

Siobhan continued to eye him with skepticism; she wasn't buying his act.

"So, what was so bad...that she was so hurt she had to try and kill you?" she asked pointedly.

Vaegril sighed, "Now…it's really not my fault…one can't help who they fall in love with. Things like this just…happen."

The pair could hear Casius laughing before he stopped to face them, "You slept with her best friend, didn't you? You idiot…how many times does this make it? Three?"

"I did *not* sleep with her best friend," the elf challenged.

Casius raised his eyebrows.

"You make it sound so tawdry," Vaegril defended himself.

The werewolf looked down at his empty wrist as if checking the time.

"Fine," Vaegril sighed, "But it wasn't her best friend…it was her sister, Rimiya."

"Protector of the Universe! Vaegril…you didn't!" Casius cried, exasperated.

"Casius! I really think she's the one," Vaegril interjected.

"V! Listen to yourself…I know you're always on the search for the perfect woman, but, trust me, Rimiya isn't it!" Casius replied harshly as he turned, picking up the pace as Siobhan quietly watched the exchange.

"She was crazy enough to leave her life…a good life… behind to chase after that rogue sister of hers," Casius continued. "Who, by the way, I am glad didn't recognize me while I was saving your ass."

"Exactly! We have a lot in common…she understands me, man," the elf was doing his best to convince his friend.

Casius stopped cold at his words and turned back to face him, "That's why you refused to come off assignment last year, isn't it? Why you stayed here, undercover."

Vaegril hung his head.

"Does she know? Does Rimiya know who you are?" Casius demanded.

The elf looked at him, eyes wide, and nodded.

"Goddamn it V! What have you done?!" the werewolf growled, "Don't you know the danger you're in? If you so much as look at another woman...she could let the entire dark grove know you're a double agent!"

"Casius, she won't," he held his hands up in surrender, "She won't...we really are in love."

Casius growled again, turning once more to walk away. It was then that Siobhan had her lightbulb moment; she knew where she recognized his eyes.

"Wait," she touched Vaegril's arm, "You're King Vaeril's son, aren't you?"

Vaegril hung his head once more, replying softly, "If you please...I'd rather not be recognized under the Orthorion name, Miss. My father shamed the court...I'd like to forget it if I could."

Siobhan nodded and allowed Vaegril to walk ahead of her. Forgetting family shame was something she knew all too well.

25

— · —

Derek lay on the hard concrete surface of the floor barely able to move. His limbs felt heavy and numb and his mouth was a desert. His head lolled from side to side as he tried to rouse himself from the stupor. Pieces of memories of white-hot pain flashed in his brain and the skin on his chest began to tingle with discomfort. The fog that covered his mind was starting to fade and his brain became washed with his last few fleeting thoughts before he went unconscious. He remembered the hissing sound and a sweet smell in the air before his world was no more. He had been gassed, he was sure of it. He looked around the darkened room and willed himself to stand.

It took the drowsy man several minutes to become upright and as he grasped onto the bars of his cell door he shouted, "I saw you, you know! What do you want with this girl!?"

Silence was his answer. Derek didn't know who this guy was or what he wanted with *Ellie*, but it wasn't for anything good. He decided to play along.

"I swear to you...If you hurt a single hair on her...you're dead. Do you hear me!? You're dead!" he yelled.

"The Devil does not sway me," the gravely voice said just a few feet beyond the door.

"Devil?" Derek muttered under his breath.

"What devil?" he called out. Derek could hear the man's voice begin to whisper to himself and he closed his eyes to concentrate on the words.

"....Hallowed be thy name...thy kingdom come, thy will be done ....on Earth as it is in heaven..." the voice was soft.

Derek frowned in the darkness.

'*The Lord's Prayer?*' he thought.

He hadn't heard that said aloud since he was a child. He remembered Mrs. Addeman, his third foster mother, and her adherence to her Sunday school teachings. She was an older, kind woman whom Derek often found to be more grandmotherly than motherly. For one fleeting moment in time, he hoped the woman the foster kids affectionately called "Mama A", would adopt him, providing him with the love and attention a little boy of ten needed. But, as it turned out, Mama A was just a short-term home and no one got to stay for long.

The man's whispering stopped to speak to Derek, "You know the verse, Devil?"

"What?" he asked.

"Rebuke your evil ways, Devil! The kingdom of God is the way and the light!" the man yelled.

'*He's calling me devil,*' Derek thought.

"Submit yourselves, then to God. Resist the Devil and he will flee from you," the man's voice declared.

Derek wasn't one for biblical literature, but he recognized that as scripture also. Who was this guy? He knew for sure that none of the Hidden tribes, courts, or packs prescribed to any sort of Christian faith; that was entirely a human condition. He searched his mind for any inkling of who his captor could be and it had all the earmarks of an attack from a recent foe. But just when he thought he had it all figured out, now this. Why was this guy so obsessed with this *Ellie*? What did this poor woman, whoever she was, have to do with this?

No one instantly came to the forefront for him. But, he had to admit his head was still cloudy from whatever gas had been used on him, not to mention the throbbing and burning in his chest. Derek was angry; not only at this man who was threatening an innocent, but also at himself because he allowed the man to get the jump on him. Unfortunately, he didn't seem to be the type to be reasoned with and Derek had to try another approach.

"Look, mister...you think I'm the Devil? Maybe I am...but which is worse...a devil being tortured or the fanatic doing the torturing?" he demanded.

Derek heard hard footsteps approaching the cell door, and someone in a black hood appeared. But before he could let go of the bars, something hard cracked across his fingers as they held on.

"Son of a bitch!" Derek cried out, pulling his now bloody hands away.

"You will not sway me, whore of Satan," the man in black said with deadly calm as he walked away from the door.

26

— · —

"**M**essenger, the Devil is not speaking," the Old man said into the rotary phone.

"He will, son. Do not allow him to divert you from your task. The Devil's destruction must be done. Once she witnesses its demise, the spell over her will be broken...you both will ascend to sit with Him," the Pale Man replied. "Use the Holy Water. That will loosen the demon's tongue."

The phone crackled.

"Remember faithful one....be sober, be vigilant; because your adversary the devil, as a roaring lion walketh about," The Pale Man said.

The Old Man finished, "...seeking whom he may devour..."

"Precisely. Go...finish your work." The Pale Man urged.

"As you wish," the Old Man's oily smile spread across his clean-shaven face as he hung up the phone. Walking to a dirty cabinet, he opened the door and found several glass jars labeled only by a crucifix, floating inside the clear liquid. He picked up three of the fluid-filled containers, exiting the dim room with purpose.

Now, he would get the demon to talk.

***

Zivahala pushed the red button on his phone and placed it gently in his pocket. His brow furrowed in pensive contemplation for a long moment before his bodyguard's voice broke his concentration.

"Problem, sir?" the man's bass voice thick with concern.

Ziv shook his head, "No...nothing we can't handle. The demonic is proving to be a bit of a challenge for our knight. No matter."

His thoughts drifted for a moment. He was determined to see the end of this evil empire and be reunited with his queen. All the planning was starting to pay off and he was particularly proud of himself for choosing such a worthy servant. The Old Man had proved to be an asset and a laudable defender of the cause. Zivahala was certain he would feel a certain disappointment when he had to let him go. But, this was business. Nothing could come between him and his goal.

"Sir?"

"Gabriel...I think it's time for us to minister to the faithful. Once the knight fulfills his duty, we will need them to be ready to rise up against the Deceiver and destroy her," Ziv smoothed his suit as he spoke.

The bodyguard nodded, "I'll bring the car around."

"No," the incubus stopped him. "It's almost time for a meal...let's break bread with the flock. Bring me the holy water. It's time to make a miracle happen."

As the bodyguard turned to leave, Zivahala's eyes flared with blue electricity.

27

The forest started to thin as Casius, Siobhan, and Vaegril approached the rundown buildings of the dreary settlement. Before making their final egress from the protective cover of the last few pines, Casius crouched low and watched. Vaegril leaned his thin back on a large tree, watching his friend closely.

"What is it?" he said aloud. Casius never moved, but kept his eyes scanning the distance in front of them.

Siobhan knelt beside him, "What do you see?"

Caisus paused and cut his eyes quickly in her direction.

"Old bell tower there?" he pointed to a tall, brick structure attached to what looked like, at one time, a church.

"Yeah?" she confirmed.

"Sentry...he's watching the tree line," he sighed as he looked skyward.

Siobhan hung her head in exasperation, "Looking for our lover boy?"

"One can assume," he rolled his eyes.

"Great," she replied.

Vaegril, becoming impatient snuck closer to the pair, "Anyone want to clue me in?"

"Sure...it seems your little tryst really didn't sit well with some-one," Siobhan leaned her back against the rough bark of the tree. She pointed over her shoulder at the crumbling bell tower. The elf squinted then opened his eyes wide as he refocused his vision. He saw the pointy-nosed Fae as clearly as he saw Siobhan.

"Well, damn," he muttered. "What do we do now?"

"Diversion," Siobhan suggested as she pushed by Vaegril, her body just skimming his.

Casius frowned, "But what kind? The three of us need to get to the other side of that town and in the dark portal together."

"Me...I'll be the diversion—" but before she could finish the sentence Casius cut her off.

"No way! That's suicide," he charged.

"Jesus, Casius! You act like I can't handle myself," Siobhan protested.

"Von...I can't let you," insisted Casius.

"I wasn't asking for permission," she growled over her shoulder, stepping into the open field.

<h1 style="text-align:center">28</h1>

Siobhan walked confidently through the grassy expanse but as she neared the back bar from the night before, she found herself surrounded by a half dozen Fae and Elves holding a collection of handguns and bows all pointed at her. She stopped instantly, eyeing the group. They began to split the circle in front of Siobhan as the tall and lanky form of Sillia sauntered forward. Her long, black hair was braided at her nape making her neck look even more elongated. She wasn't carrying her bow, but Siobhan assumed Sillia thought she had enough firepower for the moment.

"Who are you?" Sillia's thick voice demanded.

Siobhan raised a brow at the elf, "Depends who's asking."

A dangerous smile crept over Sillia's grim face showing a mouthful of teeth that looked to have been sharpened to points.

"You have balls, my friend," Sillia remarked.

"Yeah, I've heard," Siobhan replied dryly. "Is there a reason you've blocked the road?"

The elf stepped closer, "As a matter of fact, there is."

***

"So, are you just going to let her stand against Sillia by herself?" Vaegril looked shocked.

Casius jabbed a finger in his direction, "You don't start with me! If you learned to keep your dick in your pants, we wouldn't be in this mess. And...if you'll recall, I didn't have a choice."

The werewolf's mind raced as he tried to figure out their next move. He worried that Siobhan's single-minded determination to find Derek would be her undoing. Casius would never forgive himself if something happened to her.

"All I'm saying is that your girlfriend there is on the edge. You saw the look in her eye back at the barn...she was this close to nicking you in the throat with that damn sword," Vaegril held up two fingers centimeters apart.

Casius surveyed their surroundings, "She's not my girlfriend, you ass. And yes, I noticed."

He looked around for any way for them to bypass the group in the field. There was a hundred yards between the edge of the forest and the back of the ramshackle bar. The road ran along the west side of the town, heading north. But, to the east, the pines formed enough cover for them to possibly reach a rocky outcropping that ended right behind another dilapidated building. He quickly devised a plan and turned back to Vaegril.

29

—·—

"Well, is someone going to tell me, or is there some sort of secret handshake I need to know," Siobhan pressed, feigning boredom. She hoped Casius had been able to find a way into the shabby town before Sillia got fed up with the ruse.

"We're looking for someone...a slinky piece of trash named Vaegril. You know him?" the elf paced a circle around Siobhan.

"Nope," she lied.

"You sure? Because you're the sort of tarte that's right up his alley," Sillia's lip curled in distaste.

"What's he look like? Maybe I've seen him," Siobhan offered.

Sillia grinned, "Well...he's elf. Wretched dresser. Arrow hole in his shoulder."

The entire group laughed and snickered at her description.

"Huh," Siobhan grunted. A long pause fell between the women before she spoke again.

Siobhan narrowed her eyes, "What happened? He fuck your sister or something?"

"What would you know of it!?" Sillia snarled in Siobhan's face, spittle flying. Siobhan never moved, she only continued glaring at the dark elf.

She curled her nose, "Nothing. But I may have seen your boyfriend...earlier today." Siobhan threw a thumb over her shoulder, "Group of buildings, in a barn just up the road."

Sillia, still panting with fury, looked Siobhan up and down, "How do I know you're telling the truth?"

"Believe me or don't...I don't really care," Siobhan shrugged. "But if it's proof you need, I pulled these off the body."

She reached behind her and pulled a matching set of pistols from her waistband. The guns were exceptionally small with intricately engraved handles of ivy motif. Sillia's eyes widened at the sight of the small firearms.

"You recognize them?" Siobhan asked.

"I think I'll be taking those, *friend*," Sillia reached for the pistols.

Siobhan narrowed her eyes on the elf again and clenched her hands around the tiny guns, "I'm not your friend...and you can't have them."

She moved to walk past Sillia when a short Fae man, who was missing an eye, cocked his gun at Siobhan and stepped forward. The tall elf put a bony hand on Siobhan's shoulder, stopping her.

"I'm going to have to insist," she growled.

With sharp, deadly accuracy, Siobhan took a quick step back, and spun, her boot making a sickening cracking sound as it met Sillia's face. She immediately dropped to a knee and drew down on the one-eyed Fae, shooting him in both knees. As he crumpled in screams of agony, she pulled the trigger on two other Fae, who held firearms on her, in the hip and shoulder. In the excitement of the moment, the rest of the group stood in shock but then fumbled with their poorly made quivers as they reached for more arrows. Siobhan took off in a dead run across the rest of the expanse and into the back door of the bar.

"Shit!" Casius exclaimed as he watched the scene play out before them.

He turned to Vaegril, "Listen to me...Keep low. If you can keep to the trees and follow them along to that outcrop of rocks," he pointed just to the left of where the group surrounded Siobhan. "You can make it to that building...it looks deserted... wait for us there."

Casius turned making a mad dash toward the fighting.

"Where are you going?" Vaegril called out.

"Just get to that building!" Casius yelled.

Vaegril nodded and began sneaking his way quickly along the edge of the woods.

Siobhan made it through the decaying room that functioned as a kitchen then out into the common area, running right into the enormous werewolf, Ruct.

"Hey! Pretty thing...you left me hanging last night...I don't see your boyfriend around to protect you," his breath was heavy with alcohol. Siobhan stared in disbelief for a second because she was sure this maniac had been left for dead.

"I don't have time for this," she muttered under her breath as she grabbed Ruct's left hand off her arm, twisted hard, promptly breaking his wrist. He held onto his broken hand as Siobhan's thick combat boot made solid contact with his manhood. It wasn't an elegant blow, but it was effective.

The werewolf howled in pain, "You bitch!"

"You'll live!" Siobhan yelled over her shoulder as he reached for her running out the door. She stopped short when she realized she was completely surrounded by the doormen from the night prior.

"Well, look who it is boys," the enormous elf chuckled. "Where's your friend? He owes me...but, I guess you'll do as payment."

He lunged for her just as she made to grab Liarshank. But as she reached her hand back, someone grabbed ahold of her and held her with her arm pinned behind her back. She struggled to move but whomever it was had her in a vice. The group of elves laughed.

"She's awful pretty, huh Tanyl?" the one on the leader's right snickered. Siobhan noticed his fingernails were dirty and one of his eyes drooped lazily.

The leader, Tanyl, got close to Siobhan and smelled her hair, "Mhmmm...very pretty." He leaned closer to her ear, "We don't get a lot of your kind around here."

He ran his finger down her face and licked it.

Siobhan's eyes narrowed, "Touch me again...and you won't live to regret it."

"Is that so?" he replied as he backhanded Siobhan across the mouth. A trickle of blood began to flow from the broken flesh of her lip. Tanyl's dirty breath was hot against her face as he put his tongue on her cheek and slowly licked her.

A small *pop* was all that was heard before Tanyl stumbled backward, a look of shock spreading across his face as he saw the small pistol just at hip level in Siobhan's right hand. Before he could turn and show his cronies what happened, Siobhan dropped to her knees, sliding out of the grip of the elf holding her from behind.

Pop! Pop!

Two more shots rang out as she spun, shooting her captor once in the chest and once in the head. She shoved the small gun into her pocket and pulled out Liarshank. As she swung down, she caught another rouge elf in the shoulder, leaving a bloody gash all the way to his hip. She swung Liarshank again and sliced the throat of a fourth elf. A fifth one raised his hands in surrender and began to back through the door, away from the advancing woman. Once through the doorway, he turned and ran.

Siobhan jumped out of the threshold, her feet never touching the portico, and landed on the dirt road; the remaining Elves sitting at the door barely taking notice. In the near distance, she could hear Sillia's voice barking orders angrily. Siobhan took off in a dead run down the dirt road as she heard advancing footsteps behind her. The faster she ran, the closer they seemed to gain on her. She spun around looking for somewhere to hide when she heard a familiar voice.

"Von! Wait! Goddamn it Von!" Casius yelled, but she continued to run. Once he was close enough, Casius grabbed her shoulders, shoving her through the tiny doorway of a small brick building.

"I said to stop!" he yelled, panting. "What the hell is wrong with you?"

She glared at him, but never spoke as she tried to catch her breath.

"What the hell was that?" Vaegril demanded also out of breath. "Are you trying to get us all killed?"

"Get out of my face!" Siobhan screamed, anger dripping like venom.

Casius looked between the pair, "Everyone relax."

Vaegril never took his eyes off Siobhan, "Get the human under control or we're all going to die here."

Casius held up his hands as Vaegril backed away, furious and frustrated.

He faced Siobhan, eyeing the bruise that began to form around her mouth, saying softly, "You really need to stop...what's gotten into you?"

It was then that he felt the rage emanating off of her like summer heat on blacktop. Siobhan's insides trembled and she felt like she may explode. She was angry and running on little sleep. The only thoughts that filled her mind were about Derek.

"I will do what I have to do to get him back, Casius," she snarled through clenched teeth.

"Even if you get hurt in the process?" he snapped back harshly, pointing to her face.

"I will do what I have to—"

"You need to take a beat. Just stop," he ordered, pursing his lips.

"I can't!" she screamed at him. "I can't...I can't stop! All this has been a goddamn wild goose chase! I will die to get him back if I have to! No one will stand in my way."

The tears came in waves as Casius grabbed onto her shaking body, pulling her into him.

"I won't let that happen, Von," he whispered.

She pulled away from him, wiping her eyes roughly.

He forced her to look at him, "Understand?"

"Yeah. What's the plan now?" she nodded then paused for a moment to reset herself.

Before he could answer, Vaegril stood with his hand out, "Alright...give them back."

"You're down seven rounds," she said, handing him the pistols.

"Pickpocket," he glared.

"Slut," she bit back then looked back at Casius, "So?"

He chuckled, then drew a deep breath, "We've got about a mile to go. I say we book it. I think we'll have enough cover... and you literally cut Sillia's gang in half."

Drawing Liarshank out once more, she replied, "Let's do this."

30

Derek's head swam and the room spun. He squinted his eyes as hard as he could to focus on the fuzzy form in front of him. As he tried to raise himself off the table, tension pulled him back. His head lolled from side to side trying to find what held him down. His arms felt like they were simultaneously light as air and heavy as lead weights. He blinked several times before he could just make out the leather binds that restrained his arms at the wrists to boards splayed to either side. As the seconds ticked by, his mind began to clear more and more until the world came into focus.

He saw the Man had removed his hood and was dumping jugs of clear liquid into several buckets set up in a row on the floor. Derek made no more sudden movements, but instead, took in his surroundings. He could see the room was large with a room that looked to be an office to the far right and his makeshift cell to the left. The dingy concrete floor was splattered with old oil stains. He smelled gasoline. A garage...he was in an old mechanics garage.

He raised his eyes once more and watched the man filling another bucket with fluid. Near his bare feet, Derek could see a work table lined with the instruments of torture the Man had used on him earlier. A large hunting knife, propane torch, brass knuckles, and a metal baton about two feet long. As he looked closer, Derek noticed that a silver cross had somehow been added to each item.

Who did this guy think he was? The great inquisitor?

Derek closed his eyes and started to pull energy to him. He would need all the help he could absorb to get out of that garage. He controlled his breathing and opened his hands just a little. He started to feel the tiny ball of heat that formed in his palm getting bigger...

Derek convulsed violently as he was hit with a deluge of icy water.

"Son of a bitch!" he cried out.

"Speak no lies, deceiver!" The Man's eyes glared with contempt. "Your evils will be your undoing...you will tell me what I want to know."

He moved over Derek and placed a large silver crucifix on his chest. Derek watched him closely as he went back to the buckets of water and threw another on his head. Derek spat and coughed as he tried to catch his breath.

"What do you want!?" his body wretched out of the way.

"You will tell me what I want to know," The Man growled, picking up his third bucket. He stood over Derek and poured the water in a constant stream into his face. "Submit yourselves therefore to God. Resist the devil, and he will flee from you..."

Derek fought the urge to inhale until the bucket was empty. Once the last drop was gone, he spat out what had gotten into his mouth and drew in a deep breath.

"Tell me what you want!" he choked. Derek worked hard not to drown before he could use the energy blasts he was still collecting.

"If you believe that there is one God, you do well...the devils also believe and tremble," The Man barked.

A moment of clarity washed over him like the cold water that was being poured: bible verses; The Man was reciting bible verses again.

"James," Derek coughed and the Man stopped suddenly.

"What!?" he snarled.

Derek panted, "That's from the book of James, right? Believe that there's a God and you do well...et cetera."

The Man stared at Derek briefly before bending down to pick up another bucket of water, "Unclean spirits, when they saw him, fell down before him and cried, saying, you are the Son of God."

Derek took a deep breath as the man poured the icy water slowly over his face. Derek's skin began to tingle with something familiar. He *knew* that sensation; Succubae venom. Something was different about this venom though. Derek wasn't losing control of his mind or body, yet. He could feel the faintest prickle over his skin, but it seemed as though the cold water diluted the worst of it.

He raised his head off the table, "Mark! That one is from the book of Mark...I think. Man, what do you want? Just..." He swallowed hard, "Just...tell me what you want."

The Man came within an inch of Derek's face, "Certain women, which had been healed of evil spirits...like Mary Magdalene, out whom went seven devils. How many are you, devil? Hmmm?"

Derek never moved.

"Where is Ellie!?" The Man screamed.

'Ellie?' Derek thought. *'There's that name again.'*

His eyes narrowed on the Man, staring at him intently; thoughts firing through his mind like sparks. He couldn't imagine what this man would want with this woman. If the Changelings, or any other group for that matter, were going after someone, they had the Sovereign's son as a prisoner; what could they possibly want with her? Then there was the venom. It couldn't have been a coincidence that he was using water laced with Succubae venom. And the Bible verses. The man had a serious religious delusion. Derek couldn't think of anyone that would...*Ellie!*

The sparks of internal monologue converged into one massive lightning bolt of epiphany. All at once, Derek could feel two giant balls of invisible energy form in his open palms and he held them there. He cut his eyes at the man still inches from his face. But Derek only saw bloody, red fury.

"You can go fuck yourself....*Douglas*," he snarled, discharging the energy and sending Douglas flying back several feet before crashing into the tray of instruments.

The energy blast had another unintended consequence as the bindings that held Derek's wrists to the outstretched boards broke. He quickly sat up, untied his ankles, and flew off the table. Derek scrambled to find a weapon as Douglas did the same. Weak and exhausted, Derek turned around just as Douglas faced off with him.

"Demon of the wicked," Douglas growled.

"Pot...kettle," Derek struggled to remain standing.

Douglas charged him and the men began to exchange hits, blow for blow. Douglas was like a wet blanket on the beaten Derek; heavy and hard to shake. They wrestled to the ground, both men fighting for control of the other. Looking up, Derek saw the large hunting knife just a foot out of his reach. If he could manage to get to the knife, he could finish the fight for his, and Siobhan's life.

He managed to land a blow to Douglas' right temple that stunned him and Derek crawled toward the knife. Just as it touched his fingertips, an electrical shock ran up his leg and he convulsed. Before the darkness overtook him, he watched Siobhan's father toss away the electric cattle prod and pick up the last bucket of water. The concentration of venom was much higher as Derek finally lost control of himself in the growing blackness that surrounded him.

31

— • —

"We're attempting to pull a small contingent of Brethren to keep an eye on the portal, Sovereign. No one will go in or out without us knowing about it," Captain Vena marched toward the desk, shutting the door behind her. "But reaching those in the Wilds is difficult...we're scattered to every corner."

"Good," she replied distantly, "What do we hear of Vilotta?"

"King Novus of the Green Court and Queen Irhaal of the Blue have met with High Queen Imra. It's believed they will all travel to the Wilds to pose a final appeal to the Fae Queen for a peaceful resolution," Vena explained.

"Hopefully, Imra will have better luck than the whole of the Order and Council," Julia paced the floor, her hands held tightly behind her.

"Sovereign," Vena's normally commanding voice softened, "Is there something I can do for you? I can send out for some tea or...maybe some food?"

Julia stopped short then turned to face the captain, "I appreciate the offer, Tara. I'm fine, really."

"Of course," Vena smiled sympathetically. Just as Julia resumed her path around the office, Lenias Grey swung the door open wide, leaning heavily on his staff. Julia was startled at his loud shuffling entrance.

"Oh! I'm sorry...I wasn't expecting anyone," she apologized.

"Uh...Julia, we need to talk," the old man replied, hesitation firm in his voice.

Julia cocked her head, "What's wrong, Lenias?"

He took a deep breath as he shambled closer, "I've been following up on some things with my contacts...you know...parties that keep a neutral viewpoint."

"Yes, I know," she replied as Lenias took up her path, pacing across the floor.

"Well, now, I've got to be honest with you here, Sovereign...I've got more than just neutral parties that I call friends," he explained carefully.

Julia looked at him with concern as the old man sounded more nervous than she had ever heard. Who could he be cavorting with? She didn't put anything past him mostly because Lenias was cunning and played his own game of politics. She stepped in front of him, forcing him to cease his patrol, and placed her hand gently on his arm.

"What is it, Lenias?" she asked.

"I need you to meet someone...but...but this is strictly off the record. I need your word, Milady," he begged. "Please."

The old man's eyes were watery and his gaze desperate. Whomever he was about to introduce her to, Julia knew they must be important to him. She nodded her approval.

Lenias hobbled back to the door and opened it. Julia saw Jaudon just on the other side and next to her, a rather handsome man dressed in a cheaper-looking suit and tie. She saw his hair was just starting to thin, but he wasn't nearly as old as she. He also *looked* human, but Julia knew that looking human didn't really mean that he was. The man seemed apprehensive as Jaudon led him into Julia's office.

"Sovereign, please allow me to introduce you to Sergeant Jack Rollings, one of my contacts with the Portland police department...and," Jaudon glanced over at her father-in-law. Lenias bowed his head for her to continue. "And... the de facto head of Llyre Nereid Pod."

Julia's eyes widened. She felt as though all the air in her lungs had been knocked out of her for the second time in as many days. Much like the Kiada, Nereids were thought to have been extinct for hundreds, if not a thousand, years. Her thoughts raced as she attempted to catch her breath while also maintaining her decorum. She didn't know whether to be ecstatic or angry. How long had Lenias been keeping this to himself? How many more secret clans were still in hiding? Did Lenias know any of *them*?

"Please forgive me," Julia smiled sweetly, "I thought...well...I'm sure you know what I thought."

Jack nodded, "Yes, ma'am. I'm aware that our existence has been kept secret for a long time. And honestly...I'd like to keep it that way. But, I believe my reason for seeing you is too important to not come myself."

Julia smiled again and offered him a seat across from her desk. Before anyone could speak again, she raised her arms out to her side, and closed her eyes, whispering softly, "Siopilos. Tace surdilas."

A barely noticeable shimmer of golden light spread through her fingertips and began to encase the immediate area around them in a bubble. As Julia breathed out, the bubble grew and formed a barrier inside the office. Jack's eyes filled with tension.

"Not to worry...we're completely free to speak now," she reassured him, as she slowly opened her dark eyes.

Jack swallowed hard, but continued, pulling a picture out of the inside pocket of his sport coat.

"Do you recognize this man?" he asked her. Julia took the photograph from the sergeant, eyeing it carefully.

"It looks a lot like Zivahala...he's an Incubae," she replied as Captain Vena peered over her shoulder.

"How old is this picture? Last we knew, Zivahla disappeared two years ago. We assumed he was killed during the raid that killed Daria and Alexis. At the time, it was thought that someone escaped with his body," Vena explained.

"Captain, that picture was taken yesterday," Lenias stated.

"Are you saying that the Succubae are still working with the Changelings?" Julia needed clarification.

"Ma'am, if I may?" Jack asked.

"Of course."

"Ma'am, this gentleman is part of a scheme meant to defraud unsuspecting *people* out of money. And he's run this hustle in various other states...including Florida and Georgia. He's good too...it's estimated he's bilked people out of around five million dollars. Not to mention, he's also the prime suspect in the disappearances of several members of his congregation"

Vena let out a low whistle, "Wait. Congregation...do you mean like a church?"

Jack nodded, "Yes, ma'am."

He opened a folder, drawing out more pictures and several rental receipts, "We think it works like this: they start small, offer spiritual guidance to a disadvantaged group...homeless, prostitutes, runaways. Because of what he is, he has abilities, and these people are easy marks for them...willing to believe anything. He sets up shop with his small group of new followers, which is when the real scam begins. He uses them as apostles, if you will, and sends them out to spread the word.

Before long, more affluent members join and he starts raking in the money."

"What about the people that have disappeared?" Vena asked.

Jack laid out seven missing person's flyers, "They're all on that affluent end of the spectrum. We believe they either stopped giving money or saw their leader for what he was...a charlatan."

"But how?" Vena mused. "What is the essence of the scheme?"

"He convinces them he is an angel of God," Jack cocked his eyebrow.

"Which God?" Vena let out a small chuckle.

"Judeo-Christian, Captain," Julia stated. "It's a good strategy. Unwitting, unknowing humans have no idea of the powers that our world holds. They know nothing *of* this world...Zivahla would only simply need to slip venom to a potential congregant and make them see and believe whatever he wanted. We know that Daria taught some of her group basic craft...if he used any of fifty spells, it would certainly make a devoted worshipper out of anyone that already had religious underpinnings and—"

Julia stopped short. Her blood suddenly ran cold as a singular thought washed over her and all color drained from her face. She visibly shivered and her face went blank, staring in disbelief.

"Sovereign?" Vena called out to her.

"Julia!" Lenias barked with concern, reaching for her arm.

Julia's eyes found their way back to Jack's, "This isn't about Changelings, is it?"

Jack shook his head and she closed her eyes in an effort to fight back tears of fear and rage.

"I don't understand," Captain Vena began.

Jack's voice was quiet, "After my visit with Jaudon, my partner and I were assigned an urgent notification request. Department of

Corrections apparently had a paperwork *snafu*... I went to the house and met with Theodore. That's when I started putting the pieces together."

Julia nodded her head resolutely.

"It's my theory, that this man," Jack continued, pointing to the picture of Zivahala, "Used this hustle to somehow not just gain entry into our corrections system, but manipulated it into an early release for one particular man. It would be this man, with Ziv's help, that would kidnap your son in the hopes that his fiance would come after whoever took him."

"I still don't understand," Vena's eyes darted between Jack and Julia. "This is about Siobhan?"

Julia slumped on the edge of her dark honey-colored desk, rubbing her temples, "It is. It's a vendetta that's decades in the making."

32

—·—

T he dark sedan slowed to a stop in front of the squat brick building. It was perfectly hidden between two larger edifices on either side that towered over like guards. Silas sat behind the wheel, staring at the thick fire door with crumbling gray paint. He knew the Forehilein safe house would be empty now as most all the forces had been pulled to protect the Wilds. He had made a deal with Lore to keep the refugees safe. Silas couldn't think of a better place.

He moved through the building swiftly, turning on lights and prepping living quarters for new guests. Lore told him hours before that he should be expecting the first of more than three dozen Fae to arrive in the first wave. He wondered how many waves there would be and what would happen if Vilotta found out. She wasn't the type of creature to be understanding when things were being done behind her back with her people; she would see it as a coup. For a small moment, Silas worried about what would happen to Lore.

He rounded the corner into an enormous room that held a beautifully carved conference table to find Lore shimmering into view. The Fae's ability to move within the world and suddenly appear out of nowhere was something that was a well-guarded secret. Silas watched Zhaar do it thousands of times and even after more than three hundred years, it was still a little unsettling.

"Lore. I wasn't expecting you so soon," he said.

The Fae's iridescent eyes glittered, "The situation is quite dire...I had to move quickly. Are you prepared?"

"As I'll ever be...where are—" he began as the Fae woman held a finger up. Lore closed her eyes and as she slowly opened them fifty Fae men, women, and children appeared in the room.

"*Zut*," Silas whispered in French under his breath.

Lore hung her head, "Unfortunately, I will have just as many arriving before the end of the night."

Silas thought she almost looked...sad. The revelation stunned him for an instant. Fae weren't particularly empathetic to anyone's needs or desires, except their own. But Lore seemed to actually *care* about what happened to the group.

"They'll be safe here," Silas reached out, touching her hand gently, "I gave you my word."

Lore's large, opalescent eyes gazed at his hand on hers.

"I must go back. My Queen will be looking for me soon. I will return within your hour," she said softly before disappearing as quickly as she appeared.

Silas looked around the room at the group that assembled. He still needed to check the stores of food to make sure there would be enough and get them settled in rooms. It wouldn't be near the comforts the Wild provided, but they would be out of danger. Large eyes of all shapes and colors stared back at him, most wild with anticipation.

"*Zut*," the curse in French rolled under his breath one last time as he got to work.

33

—•—

The trio jogged in the tree line just off the road stopping every few minutes to quietly listen for anyone following them. While everything seemed calm, none of them trusted the silence that surrounded them. Casius' hair stood on end as his eyes darted, looking through the lines of larch and spruce.

"We go through the portal, then what?" Vaegril asked, barely skipping a breath.

"We find Ziv...hopefully he will lead us to the Lieutenant," Casius replied.

The elf rolled his eyes, "You really think we're getting to that portal unscathed? They're moving to cover the entrance, mark my words."

"No, V...it's not going to be easy, but," Casius stopped and held up a fist to alert the other two. He squinted his eyes, stretching his vision as far as it would go. He could just make out figures in the dimming light moving ahead on the path. "Damn it."

Vaegril followed his stare, "I told you."

Casius rolled his eyes.

"We shoot our way through," Siobhan shrugged. Vaegril turned to her.

"Okay, cowboy…isn't that what your kind call them? I think you need to back off," he cut hoarsely. "Let the ones with some experience handle it, okay sweetheart?"

Siobhan slipped the hunting knife at her hip out of its sheath, and charged Vaegril, shoving him against a large pine. She held the blade against his throat.

"Call me sweetheart one more time…and I may finish what Saracin started," her voice dangerously calm as she held him against the rough bark. A sly grin began to spread across Casius' face. He knew Siobhan wouldn't really hurt him, but that she was at the end of her patience.

"Okay…enough," he put his large hands on both of their shoulders. "We need to get past whoever is guarding that doorway. We need to get closer."

Siobhan dropped the knife but never took her eyes off Vaegril. She could hear him muttering under his breath.

"Crazy human…Cas needs to get her under control…"

They jogged several more yards before stopping again. This time, Casius and Vaegril had no problem seeing the small group standing in their way.

"Shit!" Vaegril spat.

"Yeah, I see it," Casius replied.

"What?" Siobhan whispered.

Casius turned back to her, "Silia beat us here somehow…she's got her sister at gunpoint." He turned back to Vaegril, "You love her? Really?"

Vaegril looked similar to a doe, his eyes wide and wistful and he leaned hard against another tree, "I do, Cas…I really do."

"Okay then," Casius removed a handgun from the waistband of his jeans and drew back the slide, "We do this Von's way. V, you get Rimiya clear of the gunfire. I'm betting Silia isn't alone. Von…cover me."

Siobhan pulled Derek's Glock from her ankle holster and nodded. Casius and Von moved ahead in the tree line as Vaegril stepped onto the open path. Holding his hands in the air, he walked carefully toward the clearly injured Silia. When he came in clear visual range, he saw Silia point her revolver in his direction. Vaegril kept his eyes moving to the trees to see where Casius and Siobhan had gone but he lost them.

"Silia! Please don't do anything stupid now, love...it's not Rimiya's fault. If you want to blame someone, I'm here," he smiled uneasily.

"Oh...*love*," her gravely voice snarled, "I do blame you. Not that I really believed you loved *me*...I always knew you'd find someone else to play with. I just never imagined you'd betray me with my own flesh and blood."

She yanked hard on her sister's hair and Rimiya cried out in pain.

"Now...Silia...I'm asking you nicely to not hurt her," Vaegril inched closer to the women, his hands still raised over his head. The fiery pain from the arrow injury in his left shoulder screamed for him to put them down.

"You can stop right there, *love*," the dark elf ordered. "I don't think I want you much closer than that."

Vaegril froze in place and he heard Rimiya quietly whimpering. His heart was wretched. Silia twisted her fist deeper into her sister's hair and Rimiya yelped with pain. Silia began to drag the younger elf toward where Vaegril stood before forcing Rimiya to her feet. She let out another cry of agony.

She threw her sister at Vaegril, "You can have the little whore...at least to say goodbye."

Silia raised her gun at the pair, but as she did, the distinctive blast of a gunshot rang out, driving Silia back a few feet. Her eyes went wild as the hand that held her gun dropped and blood began to ooze from her shoulder. Suddenly more gunfire erupted from the surrounding woods.

"Rim...get down!" Vaegril threw himself over her and covered her body with his own. His eyes bounced for a moment looking in all directions to find the source of the fight.

"Come with me!" he yelled, grabbing her by the hand, and pulling her toward the doorway. Like ghosts emerging from a fog, Vaegril watched Siobhan and Casius tear out of the forest only pausing to return fire.

"V!" yelled Casius, "Open the damn portal!"

Vaegril dropped Rimiya's hand long enough to take a short dagger out of his waistband. He ran the blade along his palm first, then hers to make the blood offer. As Casius ran up beside the pair, Vaeril handed the knife off to the werewolf, who did the same.

"Von! C'mon! The door is open...let's go!" Casius commanded. He watched Vaegril and Rimiya disappear into the opening of the dark tunnel and disappear. The hole began to shrink quickly.

"Von!" Casius yelled again.

Siobhan raced to his side jumping on his back just as he threw himself into the fastly closing door. She clung to his neck as he ran at breakneck speed along the path. Siobhan's trigger hand was numb and she began losing her grip around his neck.

"Casius! I'm slipping!" she screamed.

"Hold on...just a little bit further," he reached behind to steady her.

Sweat and exhaustion overtook her grip as she struggled to grasp tighter. But try as she might, Siobhan continued to slip until her foot touched the path behind them. The eerie purple lights of the tunnel which had been pulsing slowly and rhythmically like a heart, began to flash faster. Through the pitch black that started to engulf the light behind them, they heard an unearthly roar, like that of a bear and the entire portal began to shake violently.

"Shit! Hold on Von!" Casius bellowed as he threw her on his back again, picking up speed.

She wrapped her whole arms around his neck once again, locking her hands around her own elbows. It felt like they were on a roller coaster as the portal seemed to come alive. It bucked and twisted in what seemed like an effort to purge the invaders from itself. The turbulent bellowing that emanated from its walls was earsplitting, but neither of them had the ability to cover their heads as Casius ran faster to its exit. Siobhan suddenly felt them sailing through the air and she clenched her eyes tight and they began to fall into increasing darkness.

34

— · —

Luther pulled into a parking spot next to a dark sedan in front of the Forehelien safe house. Eyeing the car with suspicion, he couldn't imagine who would be inside. The Brethren and the Forehelien were spread thin as it was, and he didn't know of anyone who would think to come all the way on the north side of the city to look for Siobhan and Casius.

His movement was like a gust of wind as he exited the car, and entered the building. He heard conversations about sleeping arraignments and almost as quickly caught a familiar scent: it was Silas. Luther quickly made his way to the entrance of the conference room to find Silas and the Fae Librarian speaking in hushed tones. What was more shocking to him was the variety of other Fae that stood in groups throughout the room. Luther swiftly moved to Silas's side.

"Luther!" Silas seemed genuinely surprised to see his cousin. "What are you doing here?"

Silas kept the tone of his voice steady.

Luther eyed the pair, "I might ask you the same question. What are all these Fae doing in the safehouse?"

Lore's large eyes moved between the men, but she didn't speak.

"They're refugees," Silas began.

"What?!" Luther exclaimed. "What are you talking about?"

Silas smiled kindly at Lore, "If you would excuse my cousin and me...we have things to discuss."

Lore nodded her head then glided to the far corner and spoke with a group of young Changelings. Luther gazed around the room trying to keep his polite demeanor.

"What is going on, Silas?"

"It has come to my attention that not all the Fae in the Wilds are being protected from the fighting. Is it not our duty, as Forehelien, to protect the innocent?" Silas replied.

Luther's eyes widened, "Yes, cousin...but you do realize you're also protecting Changelings?"

"I do," he nodded.

"Why, may I ask?" Luther pressed him.

"These Changelings don't want to fight...they just want to live their lives as they always have. Vilotta is on the brink of persecuting all of them for crimes of the few. We cannot allow this to happen," he explained, quiet desperation lingering on his words.

Luther thought that his cousin's pleas were indeed passionate, but he sensed there was more, "Silas...where have you come by this information?"

His cousin's eyes darted in Lore's direction.

"Are you serious, cousin? The Librarian? You realize she is the queen's right hand, do you not? What kind of game does she have you roped into?" Luther demanded in hoarse anger.

Silas shook his head, "No game...these people are in real danger."

"I'm absolutely sure you're right. And you and *she* have endangered them more! What do you think will happen when Violotta finds out? Hm?" the towering vampire snapped.

"Please, Luther, keep your voice down," Silas smiled reassuringly to a few Fae who looked at the pair during Luther's outburst.

Luther stood for a long moment in thought. He knew Silas wasn't telling him the whole story. Generally speaking, Fae were not the kind of people to reach out for help from another group. The only reason they were using Brethren and Forehelien soldiers now was because they had an agreement in place with the Great Treaty. Something that benefited them greatly. Why would Lore enlist the help of a single vampire?

Luther grabbed his cousin by the arm and the pair moved like a gale through the conference room, down a corridor, and into the enormous gym.

"What did you do!?" Luther hissed.

"What are you talking about?" Silas muttered, pulling his arm out of Luther's grasp.

Luther lowered his eyes, "The Fae don't do anything unless there is something in it for them...and a deal has been brokered. What does Lore have on you, cousin?"

The moment of reckoning had arrived for Silas.

Luther knew Silas better than anyone. In an instant, Silas thought through every possible scenario in his search for a story to tell his closest confidant. This was a secret he held for more than a year. At that time, Silas did everything in his power to convince his father that the only right option was to turn Varsa over to Arvendon. His father refused him at every turn. No amount of yelling, arguments, or begging would change Dimitri's mind. He was adamantly convinced that The Hidden was safer if no one knew where she was. Silas remained loyal to his father and in return, he was lying to his friends. To his family. To Luther. That decision a year ago may get Derek killed.

Raising his hands in surrender, Silas made a choice.

"Alright...alright. I'll tell you everything."

35

They hit the pavement with a hard *THUD*.

"Uhhhh," Casius moaned. Siobhan's head was still buried in his wide chest when she realized they had stopped moving. Vaegril ran over to the pair, sprawled out on the alley's still-warm pavement.

"Hey! You okay?" he reached a hand out to help Siobhan to her feet.

Casius rolled to his side and then stood, "Yeah, I think we're okay."

"What the hell was that?" Siobhan stared behind them; a small puff of grey smoke still hung in the evening air.

"Portal collapsed. What happened?" Vaegril's eyes bounced between them with concern.

"It was my fault...I slipped," she replied, hanging her head.

"Hey...we're okay. We're all alive. But, let's get somewhere a little less exposed, huh?" Casius suggested.

The group followed the alleyway to a connecting side street that seemed less busy than the main thoroughfare. None of them wanted to draw attention in the broad daylight and even in Portland, three elves and someone that looked like an oversized human would stand out. After a quick five-minute trip, they arrived at the backdoor of Wild Inspiration.

Siobhan punched in her code and pulled the door wide allowing everyone to enter before her. The crisp air conditioning was a welcome relief to the dwindling heat of the day. She led them through the short hallway into the waiting area and offered everyone water and whatever snacks she could find. She noticed Rimiya eyeing her from just behind Vaegril's shoulder.

"I'm sorry we had to meet like this," she said softly, holding out her hand. "I'm Siobhan."

Rimiya stared at her suspiciously and nodded.

"It's alright, sweetheart...she's on our side, really," Vaegril coaxed. Rimiya's eyes softened at his voice and she gazed at him lovingly.

"Nice to meet you," her voice was like honey; luscious and sweet. She smoothed her ginger-colored hair with a thin, delicate hand. She resembled her sister, but only the best parts. She was nearly as tall as Vaegril and her eyes were an exact replica of Silia's, only friendly and full of hope. Her smile was engaging and Siobhan realized why Vaegril loved her. She was everything her sister was not.

"Likewise," Siobhan smiled.

"V," Casius said, "You and Rimiya need to get back to Arvendon. My brother will want to debrief you since you've been on assignment. Tell Alder what we know about Zivahala."

"How do we get back?" he asked, looking around.

"Closet in the office to the right...it's a doorway back," Siobhan replied.

A sly smile spread on his face, "Thanks...Thief"

"Welcome...tramp," she fought back a grin.

"Where are you two going...in case your brother asks?" Vaegril asked as they turned to the office.

Casius glanced at Siobhan, "We're going to have a talk with Ziv."

After parting ways with Vaegril and Rimiya, Siobhan and Casius stepped back into the shaded alley behind Wild Inspiration. Siobhan saw the day was getting later as the shadows around them were becoming darker and longer. The spell that camouflaged her appearance would lift soon and she was anxious to find Ziv, but where would they start? There had to be a least a hundred churches just in a twenty-mile radius. She walked slowly down the pavement and then stopped.

"I have no idea where to go," she muttered.

Casius caught up to her, putting an arm around her shoulder, "It's okay…I think I know where we start."

As they stepped out of the cool shelter of the alley and onto the bright, but desolate sidewalk, Casius inhaled the warm summer air. He allowed it to fill his lungs while he cleared his mind, raising his face to the heat that slowly faded west. He paused for a moment to take in the sounds of car engines, birds, and the distant chattering of muted conversations in the surrounding restaurants and stores. He felt a familiar, small rush of blood in his muscles and he worked to push the feeling out of his mind. Siobhan watched him for a moment in curiosity.

"Something wrong?" she asked.

Casius shook his head, "No…just getting ready for tonight."

"What's that?" Siobhan cocked her brunette elf eyebrow at him.

"Full moon," he replied, a short smirk on his face, "Now, let's go find ourselves an Incubus."

36

*B*ANG!

The closet door in Julia's office made a tremendous sound as Vaegril and Rimiya came crashing into the silence spell. The small group inside the bubble stared at the pair for a moment before Vaegril saw Jaudon Grey and another man scurry out of a side door. He watched Lenias Grey, the patriarch of the Grey Clan and Casius' father, scowling at the interruption. He felt Rimiya's elegant hand tremble inside his. Julia held her hands to her face and said a word; once she did, the room exploded with sound.

"What the hell is the meaning of this?" Lenias growled.

Vaegril stepped toward Julia, bowing his head at her and Captian Vena, "Sovereign, Captain...please pardon the intrusion...I have word from Casius and his companion, the human, Siobhan."

"Speak!" the Captain commanded. At that moment, the office door swung wide as Alder Grey charged through. Vaegril bowed his head again slightly in his direction before continuing.

"What's going on?" Alder looked confused.

"We're getting ready to find out." Captain Vena nodded in Vaegril's direction, "Lieutenant?"

"I've just returned from my intelligence mission...I was brought out by Casius and a human companion, one called Siobhan," he stated.

"Human? We have Brethren reports that he was traveling with an elf," Vena questioned.

"Glamour, Captain," he explained.

"Go on."

Vaegril nodded, "While there, they were told of an Incubae by the name of Ziv that may have something to do with the disappearance of the human's betrothed...Derek Argent. It was then that our paths crossed and I told them that Ziv had left that grove weeks prior. We journeyed back through a portal together, returning home."

"If you came back together, where are Siobhan and my brother?" Alder's brow furrowed.

"Sir, we took fire escaping...once we returned, Casius thought it was best if he and Siobhan find Ziv and we return here," Vaegril said.

"Who is this?" Alder demanded.

Vaegril gripped Rimiya's hand, "Rimiya Kaven...my mate."

"Sister of Silia Kaven?" Vena eyed the woman.

Rimiya swallowed hard, "Yes, Captain."

"Huh," she huffed. "I'll want to talk to you later."

"Where are they headed," Julia's voice was overly calm.

The elf shook his head at the Sovereign, "I don't know ma'am...All I can tell you is that Ziv likes nice things...material things...and running scams..."

"We're aware of his involvement," Vena said flatly, not taking her eyes off Rimiya. The younger elf felt uncomfortable with the captain watching her, but she understood the mistrust.

"You know about Ziv?" Vaegril frowned at the Captain, then Julia.

The Sovereign sighed heavily, "We were recently apprised of the situation."

She paused, "Lieutenant, I have to know...how is Siobhan...is she okay?"

"Yes, ma'am...very. She's unlike any human I've met, actually," he nodded. The tension in Julia's shoulders seemed to be lifted a bit at his words. Siobhan was at least alive and well, which is all she could hope for at the moment.

37

"Anything from that guy?" Siobhan asked impatiently. She and Casius had been scouring the alleys and side roads of Portland for more than two hours talking to every homeless person they came across. She was beginning it was a waste of time as most of the people thought they were either cops or scared at the sight of a woman in all leather and a giant man. She eyed Casius closely as he jogged to catch up with her.

"Actually, yeah," he replied, jamming his thumb behind him, "He thinks he knows who we're looking for. Said a really pale man in a nice suit who was asking a few of them about an old garage a few weeks back...thought it was weird. Then, he and his buddies find out about a new soup kitchen that just opened up...they walk in, and he sees the Pale Man again doing...magic tricks. Might be our guy."

"Finally! Where is this Pale Man?" her voice rose in excitement.

"Southeast Eightieth Street," Caisus smiled, "You got a car nearby?"

Casius and Siobhan returned to the studio and picked up Derek's Jeep. It took the pair thirty minutes to make their way across the city and pull up in front of the Way of Salvation Church. Casius sat pondering their next move for what seemed like hours.

"Casius...let's go.." Siobhan urged impatiently.

"I'm figuring out our move," he replied.

"What's to figure out? We go in, grab Ziv, and ask the asshole where he's got Derek," she insisted.

"Von, we can't go in and just bust down the door. We need to know he's even in there first of all...and we don't know if he's alone," Caisus objected.

She knew he was right. If the building was a nest of Succubae, they could be in serious trouble. While Ziv's venom wouldn't have any effect on Casius, she could be incapacitated.

"Fine," she slumped in the driver's seat, "We wait."

They didn't have to wait long as a black Suburban with heavily tinted windows drove beside them on the street, turning into the drive of the church. Siobhan sat up in the seat and she watched Casius bristle. Their eyes watched the truck until it stopped near the rear of the building. A man with sandy brown hair, wearing a dark suit and sunglasses exited the vehicle on the driver's side, then immediately opened the back door. Zivalah's shock of white blonde hair shone brightly in the fading summer sun and his expensive suit was a stark contradiction to the obvious poverty-stricken sight of the neighbor-hood. The two men walked to the back of the church and disappeared.

"Well, that didn't take long," Casius said.

"Zivalah? Well...Vaegril was right about him liking expensive things," Siobhan muttered. "That ride isn't cheap."

Casius and Siobhan exited the Jeep, crossing the street at an angle. Sneaking along the edge of the red brick building, the pair made their way along its outer wall until they came to the back corner. Casius peered around the edge but saw no one.

They quietly climbed the concrete steps, silently opening the or-nate wood door. Siobhan was careful not to allow it to slam against the frame. The interior smelled of old wood and musty cloth. The thin red carpet that covered the entirety of the floor was worn and shaggy. Fluorescent lights hummed above their heads as they continued further into the sanctuary.

Aged pews sat in rows on the left and right of the large space, making way for a wide aisle in the middle. The same old carpet covered the floor but the walls looked to be freshly painted. The temple itself was plain and undecorated until the eyes met the focal point of the room.

The lectern looked to be made of pure ebony and seemed to be carved with depictions of religious iconography. It was oversized for the area and a large can light hung directly over where the speaker would stand; casting down like a light from heaven.

"I don't know about the rest of the place," Siobhan whispered, "but that pulpit looks expensive."

Casius nodded, "I was thinking the same thing...impressive."

"I wonder..." she started to say when Casius raised his finger to his lips, pointing to a side door, just off the stage.

He heard voices getting closer and he wanted to hold on to the element of surprise a moment longer. He motioned for her to follow him and they flanked either side of the door and waited. Siobhan could hear two sets of feet climbing stairs just on the other side, and she drew her gun.

As the door opened, Casius grabbed the first person by the shirt, hitting him squarely in the nose. The man yelled out, grabbing his face as blood poured to the ground. Before Ziv could react to what had just happened to this bodyguard, Casius took him by the neck with his left hand, pinning him to the wall. He held his right one out to keep Siobhan from getting too close.

Siobhan's understanding was clear. She aimed for the center of the Incubae's forehead, keeping her distance.

"You must be Ziv," Casius growled.

Ziv's wide eyes stared at the pair closely.

"What...do...you want?" he choked.

"You have something of mine and I want it back," Siobhan demanded carefully.

He tried to shake his head, but Casius' grip was like a vice, "I don't—"

"The Sovereign's son. Where is he?" Casius snarled.

"I don't...know..." Ziv strained to make his voice heard.

"I'm not asking again. Tell me where he is!" Siobhan yelled.

Ziv's eyes widened more as his already pale face began to turn a faint blue hue.

"Casius...don't kill him. We need him alive," her voice broke with desperation. Casius slowly loosened his grasp on Ziv and color began to brighten his cheeks.

The incubae gasped, "I don't have him."

The bloody man on the floor moaned, waking up. He made it to a standing position and staggered drunkenly toward Siobhan.

She glanced at him and back at Casius, "He human?"

"Yeah."

"Okay," she replied, placing her weapon in her belt at the small of her back. Taking a step back away from the bleeding man, she pivoted, landing a roundhouse kick to his head. The man crumpled to the floor. In one effortless movement, Siobhan took the gun out of her waistband, pulled back the slide, and pointed it directly at Ziv.

"Last chance. Oh, and so you know...blessed bullets," she narrowed her eyes on him dangerously.

Ziv's eyes darted from Casius to Siobhan's. He studied them carefully before a tense grin crossed his face. It was a look that unnerved the pair.

"I see Julia is calling out all her forces for her little man," he smirked. "Am I to guess you two are of the mighty Forehelien Charge? I thought your the little Changeling problem would be keeping you all busy."

Casius slammed Ziv's head against the wall and the incubus began to laugh.

"I see not busy enough."

"She's not playing games you piece of shit...that's a real gun with real sanctified bullets in the chamber. I'd start talking," Casius bellowed.

A shadow of fear quickly moved across Ziv's face as he considered his options. But instead of conceding defeat, maniacal, wild laughter grew from his chest, bursting from his lungs.

"You're bluffing," he laughed. "If you kill me, you'll never find out what happened to His Highness...or his Jezabel mate. She's the one you should be looking for."

A look of confusion crossed Siobhan's face and it didn't go unnoticed by Ziv.

He guffawed louder, "Well, well, well...seems you're missing a few pieces of the puzzle."

Casius's grip tightened on the throat of the incubus until he was silent once more. Ziv's pale eyes rolled and his body was going limp. Casius opened his hand and allowed the incubus to slide down the wall, regaining consciousness once more. As Ziv came too, he looked up to see Caisus and Siobhan standing over him.

"See? You need me alive," his voice hoarse. "Maybe we can make a deal."

"Probably not," Siobhan shook her head and fired her weapon.

38

—•—

"**W**here would they go? Anyone?" Captain Tara Vena growled, stomping her combat boot on the ground. "Vaegril...did they give any indication where they were headed?"

The alley behind Wild Inspiration was nearly black but he could feel the Captain's eyes on him.

"I've never had a run-in with the Incubus. All I know about him is what I've heard in passing while undercover...he's money hungry...always buys the best...thinks humans are gullible," he shook his head in frustration not understanding why she was so angry with him.

"Damn it!" Vena yelled. The door to the studio banged shut behind them, and Vena turned in time to see Alder Grey, fully transitioned into his wolf form, standing behind them.

The man was exceptionally large in broad daylight, but in full moonlight, he was astoundingly huge. His sandy-colored hair which was normally long, yet tidy grew into an unkempt mane of sorts that followed his spine, and his ears elongated to near elf-like at the tips. His hands had turned knotty at the joints, the fingernails coming to long, deadly points. The transition also broadened his jaw, making room for canine-shaped teeth and his eyes were like orbs of gold, reflecting all light they could pull into them.

"Alright, Grey...it's all you," Vena raised her chin.

Alder sniffed the night air. He could smell a trace of his brother's scent, along with Siobhan's. He walked to the sidewalk, taking in another deep breath, then turned to the left; Vena and Vaegril followed close behind.

"Uhh...shouldn't we be in disguise? Or something?" Vaegrl commented as he trotted alongside Captain Vena.

"Why?" she snapped.

Vaegril's eyes widened, "I guess you haven't noticed the seven-foot werewolf we're following? In Portland Known. In *public*?"

"Hey! Nice costume buddy!" Someone shouted from across the street.

Tara cut her eyes in Vaegril's direction.

"Yes, ma'am. Loud and clear," he remarked.

Moving swiftly along the lesser traveled sidewalks, the trio came upon an empty lot in an industrial area. Around a dozen people in tattered clothing milled around dragging empty boxes and pushing shopping carts full of junk. Alder stopped to sniff the air. His brother's scent was stronger here at a higher concentration.

"What is it?" Vena asked.

Alder's voice came out as a snarl, as if his tongue was too big for his mouth, "Casius...Siobhan...were here."

"A homeless camp?" Vaeril mused.

"Hell, yes!" Tara's eye lit from within. "They're on Ziv's trail...which means we are too. Nice work Casius."

She turned to Alder, "You stay here, in the shadows. No reason for you to scare these people."

Alder nodded.

"Vaegril, you're with me," she ordered.

"To do what...exactly?" he asked.

"We need to find which church Ziv is operating out of. He uses the fringes of human society to spread his...message. One of these people knows where he is," she explained quickly. "Put on a glamour...spread out...we don't have much time."

39

The pair ran across the street and approached the black Jeep. The moonlight fell on Casius as soon as he exited the church, and he found himself transitioning mid-run. When they approached the vehicle, Siobhan quickly lowered the top so he could fit inside. Jumping in the driver's seat she waited for Casius to get in.

"We need a plan," he offered, his voice distorted by his thick jaw.

"The plan is to find Derek before Ziv can dig out those bullets and call whomever he's working with," she snapped.

His golden eyes narrowed on her, "We can't go in guns blazing. We don't know how many there are or who they are. We need help...we need to call my brother.

"We don't have time for that...and we can't exactly pick up a phone can call Arvendon," she argued.

"Don't have to," Casius pointed a sharp finger to the moon overhead.

He closed his eyes and steadied his breathing. Within an instant, he felt his brother's vibrations close by. The sensation felt like waves as he pushed his consciousness further, getting a lock on Alder. Seeing through his eyes, Casius pinpointed his location. He opened his eyes and looked in all directions.

"What is it?" Siobhan ordered.

"I see them...they're at the homeless camp," Casius's grinding voice said. "I'm showing Alder where to go next."

He paused.

"They know about Ziv...something else...Ziv's partner...he looks familiar—"

"Good enough! Let's go get Derek," Siobhan turned the key and the vehicle roared to life. Pulling forward, she swung into the road, making a U-turn toward the garage.

40

They skidded to a stop a half block down from the old mechanics' garage. They noticed the windows had been painted over and there was no indication of light emanating from inside. Noticing the black van near the front door, Siobhan threw off her seatbelt and jumped from the vehicle.

"We need to wait for Alder and the rest," Casius ordered.

Drawing her gun from its holster on her side, Siobhan moved fast, checking entrances for a way inside.

"Siobhan!" Casius called after her. "Damn it!"

He bounded after her but as he rounded the corner into the alley, she slipped into a side door. His attention was drawn elsewhere as his connection with Alder became stronger. He could hear Tara and Vaegril having a conversation and he knew they were close.

'Alder...I'm following Von inside...I couldn't stop her...hurry. Send backup.'

He heard Alder's voice clearly, *'Brethren contingent on their way.'*

Casius pulled the door open, stepping into the darkness.

***

Siobhan entered the building quietly, being careful to step lightly so as to soften her footfalls. She knew Ziv's partner had to be somewhere in the building, so she had to get Derek out as quietly as possible. She hugged the dirty cinder block wall, making her way around the cluttered garage and the smell of oil and gasoline was sharp in her nostrils.

It didn't take long for her eyes to adjust to the dim lights inside the building. She turned the corner from the small office that jutted out from the wall and found the makeshift cell in the far-left corner. After checking the main bay for any movement, she crept quietly to the cell door. Feeling along its edges, she found the small window, then raised her tiptoes to look inside. What she saw horrified and angered her.

Derek lay supine on the cold floor, his arms splayed to his sides. She saw the burned flesh on his bare chest, his bloodied and bruised knuckles, and a gash in his forehead. With other various bruisings over his body, she wondered if he was alive. He looked eerily pale and unnaturally still.

The thick iron arm that barricaded the door creaked as she lifted it, moving it away. She checked the threshold for a trap before entering the cell and then quickly knelt next to Derek. She brushed the hair from his face, whispering to him.

"Reek? Reek...it's me...can you hear me?" she felt a wave of relief when Derek winced as she touched his head.

As he opened his eyes, he frowned for a moment looking into her face. It dawned on her that she still wore the glamour Saracin had given her nearly twenty-four hours prior. But before she could explain, Derek lifted his hand to touch her cheek.

"If I'm dying, and you're an angel...give the eyes back to Siobhan. Those belong to her," he smiled weakly. Tears gathered on Siobhan's face as she bent to kiss him on the lips.

"Baby, it's me...it's Von," she whispered.

Derek blinked slowly, then smiled at her, "There you are...I see you now."

He reached up with a dirty hand, touching her face again. Siobhan realized he was playing with her hair and when she looked again, it was her natural auburn color. The glamour was wearing off.

She bent close to his ear, "Reek...can you move? We need to get out of here...Casius is right outside...he's getting help."

"No! No..." Derek's head shook violently.

"Reek...it's okay, the calvary's on the way–"

Derek grasped her hand as he scrambled as best as he could to his feet. He was unsteady and weak, his knees giving out as he desperately tried to stand. His face reflected a frantic fear that she found concerning and confusing. As he steadied himself, he grabbed onto her shoulders tightly.

"Von..." his voice was raspy and strained, "Your father—"

Suddenly, a voice behind Siobhan bellowed, "Ellie...is that you? What are you doing? Come out of there Ellie!"

Siobhan froze as a bolt of fear and panic shot through her entire body. His voice slid over her like a thick poison and the tears that had been hanging in her eyes after she discovered Derek now fell as a product of abject terror. Almost immediately, the little girl inside her wanted to crawl into a ball and disappear from existence. The fright she felt at that moment, she hadn't felt in decades, and she almost wet herself. Her wide eyes stared at Derek in desperate horror, and she felt her entire body start to involuntarily tremble.

"Ellie! I'm talking to you!" Douglas Griffin bellowed loudly.

Rage filled Derek's face, but Siobhan shook her head at him in a warning. The pair stood together, and she turned to face her father.

Siobhan steadied her breath, "My name is *not* Ellie. Did *you* do this?"

"Your name is Eleanor Siobhan Griffin...no matter what you wanna call yourself," he barked.

"My name is Siobhan Katherine Miles...and *you* will get used to that," Siobhan snarled back bravely.

Douglas' face turned red with fury as he started toward them, "You disrespectful little bitch! It's clear you've forgotten your manners, young lady...I guess I'll just have to remind you—"

He raised his open hand to hit her.

"Stay back!" Siobhan raised her gun at his head and Douglas froze. She backed her father out of the cell's doorway as Derek limped closely behind. They all slowly made their way into the garage.

"You stay away from me...I *will* pull this trigger," she ordered.

"Ellie! You put that down!"

"My name is Siobhan!" she screamed, her voice shaking. "And you'll never touch me or my family again!"

Douglas roared with laughter, "Your *family*? These devils? I *am* your family...I am your blood!"

He raised his hands over his head, looking at the ceiling, "You're the child of a messenger of the God Almighty. And you bring shame to yourself and God when you cavort with these worshipers of Satan. You need to beg for forgiveness—"

"*You?* A messenger of God? Since when *Dad*? Is that what you found in prison? Another bible? All these years and you still haven't read it, have you? You're still the same pathetic psycho," she spat.

Douglas looked skyward, raising his arms in the air again, "I have met an angel of the Lord."

A light went off in Siobhan's head and everything started to make sense. The church. The light above the pulpit.

Ziv had been a member of Daria's nest and she knew magic. The thoughts rushed like a river. Ziv had convinced her father that he was an *angel*. Ziv took a homicidal man with religious delusions and turned him into a weapon. It was all coming together.

"You were suckered! Zivahala is an Incubus who did a few tricks to manipulate you. They want Derek and me dead! You got played *by* the devil, *Dad*," she glowered.

He stared at her for a moment in thought.

Siobhan shook her head, "You just can't see it, can you? You'll never be able to see what you've done. Why?! Why did you do this? Why can't you leave me alone!?"

Hot tears formed in her eyes, "Why do you hate me so much?"

"Von, don't. He's not worth it," Derek put his hand on her shoulder, whispering.

Douglas glared at him, pointing his baton at Derek's face, "You stay out of her head, Devil."

"Shut you're fucking mouth," she steadied the gun pointed at his head.

"How dare you speak to me with such...filth. I raised you to have respect...I raised you to know your place," Douglas charged.

"You raised us to be fearful! That's what happens when you call your children stupid... worthless... and brainless. It's what happens when you starve your children and force them to watch *you* eat so you can teach them about gluttony. It's what happens when you beat your children bloody for leaving toothpaste on the sink! Do you remember, *Dad*? Cleanliness is next to godliness, right?" she charged forcefully.

Derek stared from Douglas to his fiancé. He knew Siobhan had lived a nightmarishly difficult life and that her father was dangerously abusive, but in the entire decade they knew each other, she hadn't described in as much detail the exact events that had taken place. Derek couldn't help but see a tiny, frail red-headed little girl in his mind. An innocent, scared little girl. A little girl who could be *his* daughter someday. He saw his goddaughter, Nerissa's, face. The thoughts made his blood boil. He could feel the air around him crackling with energy. He wished he had the strength to pull it together. Derek put his palms out in a desperate attempt to gather what he could.

"Von...what are you talking about?" his eyes narrowed on her father.

"Oh...Reek, this is Father of the Year here," she glowered at Douglas. "Do you remember how I lost my first tooth? Because I do. I lost it after you punched me in the mouth for throwing up on the floor when I had the flu! Spare the rod and spoil the child, right *Dad*?"

Siobhan was sobbing so loud her throat hurt. With each word, she took a step closer until the muzzle of the gun was inches from his forehead. Douglas's eyes never moved from the barrel. Derek kept pace with her but as she took her last few steps, he tried to pull her back. He knew she was getting too close.

"*You* were supposed to be a protector...that's what real dads do! Do you know what all of those beatings and starvation and abuse got me? A dead mother. A dead brother...and one piece of shit boyfriend after another. The last one...oh...the last one...you would have liked him, *Dad*. He liked to beat me too," she cried.

'*Paul,*' Derek thought. He remembered how he felt three years prior when he and Theo realized something was wrong in her relationship with the television reporter. Derek wanted to kill him. The rage continued to build, and Derek didn't know if he would be able to contain it much longer. He tried focusing the energy in his palms but was still unsure if he could hold onto it.

Siobhan continued, "But you know what? I came out okay in spite of all of that. I have a family who loves me...I have friends who have my back...and I will have a husband who has already been to hell and back for me. So you...you can go straight to hell and fuck yourself, *Dad*," Siobhan stood resolute.

The debilitating terror of facing him had turned to stone-cold fearlessness. She held nothing back. The state of catharsis that washed over her was unlike anything she ever felt before. This would be the end; she was sure of that.

Douglas was quiet for a long moment.

"I see.... I see what's happened here. You...you've become the Whore of Babylon, haven't you?" he quipped. "You're already one of them."

"You son of a bitch!" Derek charged toward him, but couldn't gather the force to throw his way.

"No! Derek! He's not worth it," Siobhan pressed into him to stop his advance.

Douglas tilted his head, "They've taken you."

Suddenly, Siobhan's father made a quick swipe with his baton, knocking the gun from her hand. Derek made a limping run to grab it as Douglas wrestled with his daughter.

Siobhan shoved her father away from her, throwing him off balance for a split second. Holding the small bat, he swung it deftly at her head but missed. He swung again but Siobhan blocked the blow with her left forearm while knocking him in his chin with a right fist uppercut. Douglas looked surprised as he quickly cradled his face and readied to square off with his daughter once more.

As he lifted the bat to take another swing, his arm was pinched in what felt like a vice. Douglas turned to look up into the golden eyes of Casius Grey, a full-moon werewolf.

Casius squeezed the man's arm and Siobhan could hear the bones popping and cracking as they broke. She couldn't tell if her father was screaming in pain or in fear of the towering creature that held him. As Casius threw Douglas to the ground, Siobhan backed away until she found Derek again. Derek picked the gun off the ground and pointed it at the writhing man.

"You will never...*ever*...darken our door again. Do you hear me?" his voice was rough like gravel. "You will *never* see Siobhan again...or I promise I will put a bullet in your fucking head."

Douglas laughed through grinding teeth, sweat, and tears, "Babylon can have its whore."

As if in slow motion, Douglas reached into his waistband, and pulled out the hunting knife, raising it over his head. Derek moved quickly to put himself between Douglas and Siobhan and just as he started to pull the trigger of the gun, an ear-piercing scream echoed off the walls of the garage. The wet squelch of torn tissue and the familiar stench of blood permeated the area as the screams were immediately silenced. A look of shock spread as fast as the blood on his shirt as Douglas fell forward.

Derek, still holding Siobhan, turned in time to see Casius drop the windpipe out of his claws; his mouth locked in a snarl and his eyes wild with ferocious anger. Derek held Siobhan tightly for several minutes as he felt her shudder with tears and screams into his chest and she clung to him with every inch of her body. She knew it was over and that her father would never hurt anyone again. Derek was severely injured, but he held her until emotion overtook her body and she started collapsing to the floor. Casius stepped over Douglas's lifeless body to steady Derek before sweeping Siobhan into his arms and helping the pair out of the building.

Once outside, the trio was swarmed with Brethren medics and guards. Derek leaned on a tall elf as she helped him limp into the back of a nondescript van. Casius stepped inside with Siobhan still in his arms, laying her on the gurney. Derek curled himself around her, pulling her in close.

"Casius are you alright?" Alder asked impatiently noticing the blood. Tara looked inside the vehicle.

"The target is dead," he reported coldly.

Placing a hand on his shoulder, Vaegril was careful with his words, "It's okay Casius...you did the right thing."

"Tara," Alder barked, "Derek? Siobhan?"

"Both alive," she replied, shutting the doors.

Casius turned to the medic, "Get them to Arvendon. We'll alert the Sovereign they're on the way."

"Casius, we need to get out of here...we can't be here looking like this," Alder suggested, gazing into his brother's eyes. "Tara, Vaegril put on your glamours...your contact will be Jack Rollings. He'll know what to do."

"What about Ziv?" his brother demanded.

Tara nodded curtly, "The incubus is in custody. Probably already in an interrogation room...Casius, please, You and Alder need to go."

The men squeezed into Derek's vehicle, driving into the night as police sirens screamed in the distance.

41

— · —

Silas and Luther's footsteps fell in unison, bouncing off the stone walls as they marched the corridors of Chateau Blanche. The pair would finally put an end to the madness Dimitri set about. They would take Varsa, by force, if necessary. For the first time, in a long time, Silas felt a sense of relief. He would finally be able to uphold his faithful pledge to The Hidden and its treaty. The cost could potentially be great, but if it meant an honorable end, he would do what he had to.

As the pair made their way to the east wing, Silas replayed his confession over and over in his mind.

"...Dimitri took her...she's at the chateau..." he told Luther.

"This whole time?" his cousin replied.

"My father can't be reasoned with. I've tried," Silas explained.

"You made a deal with a Fae!?" Luther's baritone voice echoed off the gym's walls.

As they reached the entrance to the dungeon level, Silas used his key card in the electronic lock. It made a beep and the door unlocked. The men hurried down the circular stone stairwell, reaching the second security door. The hair on the back of Silas's neck stood on end; something didn't feel right.

He stopped just inside the door, "Luther...does this seem right to you?"

"What?"

"Father's had guards posted at every door the entire time she's been here," Silas's eyes darted around the hallway.

Understanding washed over Luther, "There's no one here."

"Exactly," Silas and Luther locked eyes before sweeping down the corridor of cells. Once they reached Varsa's they slowed to tactical movement. They moved like a machine, zig-zagging in front of each other until they reached Varsa's open cell door. Silas stepped inside, finding something that sent shockwaves through him.

Varsa's body lay on a table of steel, her arms and legs strapped by leather shackles. Bolted to the right side of the table was a hinged, razor-sharp blade, much like a scythe, placed over her throat. The pair recognized it as an updated version of an old Polish anti-vampire device. The person risked injury, but most likely, death if they attempted to move or stand from the table.

Varsa's head lay on the floor.

Luther walked in slowly, taking in the scene, "What in the hell—"

"*Merde*!" Silas exclaimed.

"Do you think...Dimitri?"

Silas shook his head violently, "No...he wouldn't. Would he, Luther? No, she did this to herself...even in death, she's exacting her revenge."

"I don't understand," Luther's brow furrowed.

Silas turned to his cousin, "Don't you see? This is my mother's final 'Fuck you!' She gets what she wants...to become a martyr for her cause and eternal adoration. My only question is why my father would put her in something like this...knowing her the way he did."

Silas was trying to convince himself as well as his cousin.

"That's a question we will ask when we find him. But for now...what do we do with her body?" Luther asked.

Silas, gazing into Varsa's cold eyes, thought for a moment, before replying, "I'm going to...what's the term the humans use? Go old school."

42

—·—

The Hidden's stronghold was buzzing with activity for several days after Derek's rescue. He and Siobhan spent a minimal amount of time in the infirmary, just long enough for him to get his wounds treated, and then were escorted to their private quarters. After several days of isolation together, Derek finally emerged to debrief with the Order. As he walked down to the Conclave chamber, running into Casius. His friend looked different. He was solemn; sad, even but still greeting Derek with a smile.

"Hey man, how you doing?" Casius reached out his large hand, pulling him in for a hug.

Derek slapped him on the back hard, smiling, "Good. I'm good."

"You look better than the last time I saw you. How's Siobhan?" his eyes lowered, reflecting the tone in his voice.

"She's getting better...seeing her father again wasn't something she ever expected. No one did," Derek admitted. "You should go up and see her...I know she'd like–"

Casius shook his head, "I don't know...I can't imagine I'm her favorite person right now."

"What are you talking about?" Derek gazed, bewildered. "Casius, you have to see her."

"I killed her father, Derek–"

"I know that...*she* knows that...she doesn't hold that against you. If anything, we're both grateful he's gone. Please, Casius...go see her," Derek prodded.

"People don't get over things like that...no matter how much they hate the person...she's never going to forget what I've done," he argued.

"How do you think it's going to make her feel when you ghost her? You're not that kind of person, Casius. I know how much you care about her...and I appreciate you being there and helping her not go completely out of her mind when I disappeared. I'm begging you...don't disappear on her," Derek replied. "She needs you...We both do."

"She...she told you that?" he asked softly and Derek nodded.

The werewolf hung his head because he knew his friend was right. How shitty of a person did it make him if he wouldn't face her? Was he really that much of a coward that he wouldn't speak to his family again? He thought about Alder and the last words they spoke to each other. He knew he had a lot of mending to do.

Derek gave him a strong pat on his shoulder, "Think about it...I've got to run. The Order is waiting for me."

"Yeah...yeah," Casius remarked as Derek walked away.

Siobhan heard a soft knock at the door as she left the bathroom. She hugged her downy soft robe around herself as she answered it. Casius' tall and broad body once again took up most of the frame of the door.

"Hey," he said softly, then took note of her robe, "Oh...I'm sorry...if this is a bad time."

"No! Not at all...please, come in," Siobhan insisted. "I was–"

She put a finger up, "Give me a second."

She went back into the bathroom and returned a minute later barefoot but fully dressed in jeans and a tee shirt.

"Hey," she said.

"I don't mean to bother–"

She put her hand up, "I'm going to stop you right there...why haven't you been to see me?"

Casius stared wide-eyed at her.

"I've waited for days...what's the matter with you?" she frowned.

Casius wasn't sure how to respond as Siobhan raised her eyebrows indicating her question was certainly not rhetorical.

He swallowed hard, "I didn't think... you would... want to see me."

"Why?" her frown deepened.

"Because of ...what happened," his voice uncharacteristically weak.

Siobhan's eyes softened as she stared for a moment at her friend. She moved toward him, wrapping her arms around his waist. He felt her love surround him as she held onto him.

"Casius...you saved Derek," she pulled away from him, "and you saved me. My father will never hurt anyone ever again...I could never be angry about that."

He realized he had been wrong and allowed her to hug him once more. When they parted, she motioned for him to sit in the chair as she took a spot on the edge of the bed, facing him.

"I do have a confession," his voice softened. "I heard what you said...what he did. With everything else I've seen...what you've let me see...I'm so sorry, Siobhan."

"Things happened the way they were supposed to...he would have killed Derek with that knife had you not... you know. And I *know* that." She hung her head, "I'm sorry you heard all of that though...I really thought I would take that to my grave."

"No...stop. You don't have *anything* to be sorry for...what he did...to you and your family," Casius shook his head angrily. "Unforgivable."

"Okay then...so we both need therapy," a slow smile crept along her face. Casius returned one of his own, staring at her for a long moment.

"So...looks like we missed your wedding date...but, I'm sure the Sovereign was able to postpone the ceremony, flowers, food, band--" he smiled.

Siobhan shook her head, "I don't know Casius...the last few days have been a lot."

"So, what are you saying? You don't want to get married?" he looked at her surprised.

She was quick to respond, "No...I really want to marry Derek...but I still wish it could be a quiet affair, you know? Sans the pomp and pageantry."

"I understand that...and I'm sure the Lady would too," he shrugged, "Just think about it."

Siobhan nodded.

"You know...I've got to meet my brother for some Charge business...You're going back to Portland tonight, right?" Casius asked, standing to leave.

She rose with him, "Yeah, Derek needs to resume his post...we'll sort the wedding stuff out soon."

He bent to kiss her on the cheek, smiling slyly, "Yeah...okay...I'll come by tomorrow...sound good?"

Siobhan smiled at her friend, shutting the door behind him.

43

—·—

The enormous room was alive with noise as groups talked among themselves about the recent rescue of Derek Argent. As he entered the circular room at Julia's side, the space became an explosion of applause. All members rose to welcome the Ascendant home. As Julia took her seat, a hush fell over the room as she waited to speak.

"Brothers and sisters...I call this Conclave to order. I believe the first line of business is the debriefing of Gold Lieutenant Argent. King Novus of the Elven Green court, you have the floor," Julia's voice boomed over the hall.

King Novus rose, "First, let me extend our gratitude to the members of Grey Pack and our own Captain Tara Vena for their tireless efforts in your recovery, Lieutenant."

Derek nodded.

"Yes...yes..." Queen Vilotta cackled. "We are so very thankful that you have been saved from the clutches of death, boy. But, tell us...for whom are we to blame for your...disappearance?"

Julia narrowed her eyes on the fae, "Your Highness, I believe King Novus still has the floor."

"Your Sovereign, it seems the Fae queen has her own agenda in mind. I concede my time...for now," he bowed to Vilotta.

Julia sighed, "Queen Vilotta of the Fae has the floor."

"We're waiting," Vilotta tapped her thin fingers impatiently on the arm of her chair.

"An incubus by the name of Zivhala coerced a human man, Douglas Griffin into my capture, Queen," Derek stated as a matter of fact.

Vilotta's laughter filled the room, "A mere human was able to capture and hold the future head of the House of Silverlight?"

Derek considered how to answer. Surely she had already been given the details of his abduction and imprisonment. How Douglas Griffin used a police baton and ketamine to knock him out for transport to the cell inside the garage. The various ways the insane man tortured him with knives, fire, and succube venom-laced water. The way Douglas kept him subdued by the use of sevoflurane, a general anesthetic used in surgery.

"Get to your point, Vilotta," Lenias Grey barked.

"My point, *hound*," her hungry eyes narrowing on the old man, "Is that while your Forehelien were being led on a ridiculous chase by an incubus and a human looking for this...*child*... the Changelings were impudent in their attacks on *my* people. A waste of resources that should have been in the Wilds! This war will not end until every last one of the conspirators is...dealt with."

"What about the ones that aren't conspiring against you?"

The gathered members turned to see Silas standing inside the door, a leather pouch strapped across his shoulders. Vilotta's pale face turned toward him and she grinned salaciously.

"Counsilor Silas...so good for the house of Montagne Blanche to make a showing," she sneered.

"I ask that you answer my question, Queen," Silas walked slowly toward his seat.

"The Changelings are seditious, disloyal..." she said.

The vampire put his finger up, "And not all of them are fighting against you, are they Queen?"

She glared at him as a blanket of silence fell over the chamber.

"As a matter of fact," Silas continued, "You have persecuted an entire sect of your own people in the name of winning your war. Fae you have sworn an oath to protect. Fae we've all sworn an oath to protect!"

Silas's voice carried throughout the still room. All eyes watched him intently.

"I'm calling for you to uphold your oath, Fae Queen, as your word is your life bond. Return to the negotiation table at once!"

A guttural snarl that sounded like it should come from a much larger creature, rose from Vilotta as her face contorted in rage, "How dare you speak to me of life-bonds! If Dimitri had taken care of his own house...the vampire poison would have never made its way to my door!"

"Ah...yes...speaking of that..." Silas swiftly pulled something the size and shape of a basketball out of his leather pouch and rolled it down the large table. When it stopped, Varsa's cold, dead eyes stared up at Vilotta. The room gasped in horror at the sight of the former vampire queen's severed head.

"A gift from the house of Montagne Blanche. Your instigator is dead. I call for you to uphold your oath, Queen...return to the negotiations. Fulfill your duty to all your people...*honorably*," Silas commanded over the clamoring of the group of witnesses.

Lore, who, until now, was sitting silently through the entire exchange cocked a delicate eyebrow, "Well, that was certainly...unexpected."

***

Julia's private chambers were buzzing with activity within minutes of the dismissal of the Conclave. In more than three hundred years of the Great Treaty, never had such a display been delivered. Julia, among others, had tough questions that only Silas could answer. And while Julia would have liked for this to be a more private matter, the wheels of gossip were already spinning.

As the final person filed into the office, Derek took it upon himself to seal the room, "Siopilos. Tace surdilas."

The soft, golden light was barely noticeable as it created a bubble that encapsulated everything in the chamber. Julia nodded her appreciation to her son before she spoke.

"Silas...you have a lot of explaining to do," she scolded the vampire.

Silas nodded his head, "Please, Sovereign, forgive the theatrics in the chamber. It was brought to my attention recently that the Fae queen was targeting Changelings in her war against them."

"We already knew that," Lenias interjected gruffly.

"Yes, sir...she said as many days ago when we were in this same room. But she was targeting all of them...even the ones who refused to turn against her. Innocent Fae. It's not right...it's not...honorable." Silas stated.

Julia lifted her fingers to her mouth in thought, "How did you come by this information, Silas."

He swallowed hard, "A...confidential informant. But someone very close to the inner workings of Fae."

Julia's eyes cut to Lenias.

"Where is Dimitri?" she continued.

"I don't know, Sovereign. I haven't seen my father in the last twenty-four hours," he shook his head.

"How did you find Varsa?" Julia's voice hardened.

"I didn't," Silas said flatly.

Julia cocked an eyebrow. She smelled a rat. Silas was skirting around her questions and she had enough of the game.

"*Where* did you find Varsa?" her voice piercing the rising tension.

He took a deep breath, "At the chateau."

Silas then did something that made Julia take pause. He blinked his eyes three times in rapid succession, then two long blinks, followed by three more quick bats.

Julia watched him carefully. "Tobias?"

"My lady...I do not know where my cousin is–" he began before Julia cut him off.

"Find him, Tobias. I feel Dimitri may have some insight to offer," she ordered.

"What about Vilotta?" Lenias asked.

King Novus stepped forward, his lips pursed in a satisfied smirk, "Funny thing about having secret agendas out in the open. They have a way of suddenly changing one's perspective. I'm told the Queen of the Fae has decided to sit down for peace talks. And...she does seem to be enjoying her new...*trophy.*"

Julia smiled cautiously, "You'll keep me apprised of the progress, Novus?"

The king bowed his head. Julia nodded to Derek to release the spell and everyone inside. While the group began to file out, Julia indicated to Derek that he needed to stay behind.

She cleared her throat, "Silas...a word?"

The vampire stopped in his tracks, turning back on his heel, "Ma'am?"

Julia nodded at Derek and he reset the privacy block. She took a deep breath.

"Do you know when I was a little girl... do you know what I dreamed of doing, Silas?" her smile now warm and motherly.

Silas shook his head watching her pace, "No, ma'am."

"I dreamed of being a soldier. I know, I know...why would a little girl...a witchling of the House of Silverlight...ever dream of being a fighter...a conscript?" She shrugged, "If you could ask my mother, she'd probably say it was despite *her*."

She chuckled to herself, "Richard...and even Alder would disagree. They would both say, I just love a good fight. But...for better or worse...that was my dream. To be a Brethren...or Forehelien, even."

She moved leisurely around the room as she spoke. Following her with his eyes, Silas stood like a statue.

"Silly dreams of a little girl...because my path was chosen already. My destiny would be not to *join* them...but to *lead* them. But, to do that...I had to think like them...even commit to memory military strategies, techniques...old and new...Hidden and *Known*," she stopped in front of him.

 Looking into his face, she blinked her eyes rapidly three times, then raised an eyebrow, "But, you knew that, didn't you?"

A slow smile spread across Silas's face; she recognized the code.

"You requested this meeting, Councilor...the floor is yours," she said, turning back to her desk.

"I offer you a confession, My Lady," Silas began. "You must know that I never wanted to deceive you."

"Was I deceived?" she lifted her brow again.

Silas stared at her blankly.

Julia narrowed her eyes carefully, "There isn't much in this place that *I* am not aware of."

"My Lady...this past year...I..." Silas stammered looking for the right words. He wanted to tell her the truth, all of it, but he feared disappointing her. Much like Dimitri had disappointed him.

"Served honorably. Everything I would expect from you," she smiled knowingly. "You're a good man, Silas of Montage Blanche. I know you've upheld your oath courageously...just as I know Dimitri did not kill your mother."

"*Merde*," he muttered and Julia looked at him with care.

"It was suicide, Silas. She wanted to make herself a martyr for her cause," she reached out, touching his hand. "I *am* sorry Silas...you've always deserved better than Varsa."

He looked down at her hand and cupped his over it.

"Thank you, Julia," he smiled, whispering softly.

She nodded.

"Now...Counsilor...I expect you to return the refugees to the Wilds as soon as a treaty is signed," she sat in her chair behind the honeyed desk.

Again, surprised by her uncanny knowledge of events, Silas smiled, "Yes ma'am."

Derek released the spell, allowing Silas to leave. He stared at his mother in astonishment.

"How did you know?" he asked.

Julia shook her head, "I didn't...not everything, at least. Dimitri is cunning and has nearly seven hundred years of experience. I suspected after a couple of months and we hadn't heard anything out of Varsa, that Dimitri might be involved. Does it technically go against the Great Treaty? Yes...but Silas didn't learn about honor and duty on his own."

"But, now she's dead," Derek stated.

"Dimitri wouldn't kill her...even though she betrayed him at every turn, I think deep down, somewhere...he still loved her. But he couldn't control her...and her ideals certainly didn't match his. He did what he had to do to keep everyone safe."

Derek chewed on his mother's words. The Great Treaty bound the houses of the Hidden together in peace, but sometimes maintaining that peace came with a cost. He realized that the laws weren't necessarily as rigid as he once thought. They were pliable, adaptable, and alive. They morphed and transformed to allow for principled action just as they could be changed for dissonance. He realized the gravity of the role of the Sovereign. They weren't just there as a figurehead and someone to turn to in times of strife. They corralled the discord and disparity; they put the ship right in stormy seas.

"Mom," he stepped toward her.

"Yes?"

"I don't know if I'm the right person to serve as Sovereign," Derek confessed.

Julia took another deep breath.

"You're right...you're not," she admitted. "Not yet, at least."

Derek looked confused, "Wait...you..agree with me?"

"Why does that surprise you?" she smiled.

"Well," he paused. "Because I thought it's what you wanted."

Julia rose from her seat, walking around the desk to meet her son, "I do...but, not yet. I still have a lot of years left before I'm ready to concede the seat. And you have a lot of years to learn from."

She wrapped her arms around him, "Son, you'll know when you're ready...no one is in any hurry."

44

—·—

The summer Portland days brought with them a sense of peacefulness that Siobhan hadn't felt in almost her entire life. She always had a feeling she was always on the edge of another fight, another mistreatment, another moment of chaos. These weren't the emotions of the strong woman she had become in her life, but those of the child she was never allowed to be.

Siobhan felt a grand release of pressure and pain in Douglas's death. She would never have to wait for the other shoe to drop again, he could never haunt her future or bring the terror and trepidation to which she had grown accustomed. She could finally take a deep breath.

Rolling onto her side, she stretched sleepily under the oversized comforter. Running her hand along Derek's muscular body, she curled tightly along his side. She gently pulled her fingers over his chest just grazing his healing burns. Moving her hand gently to his shoulder, she traced his large lion tattoo from memory.

"That tickles," he smiled.

"I know," she grinned sleepily.

Derek pulled her close, wrapping her entire body with his, "What time is it anyway?"

"Looks like twelve-thirty," rising up, she looked at the alarm clock. After returning to their home a few nights before, Derek immediately resumed his position as the Guardian of Portland and had several late nights catching up on duties. "What's on the agenda today, Sir Guardian?"

"A surprise," he smirked.

Siobhan was instantly awakened, "What kind of surprise?"

"You'll see…" he remarked as he tickled her ribs and she screamed with delight.

"What did you do?" she laughed.

Derek sighed contently, gazing sweetly into her emerald eyes, "I've made some arrangements for us…get dressed and I'll show you."

"I have a better idea," she whispered seductively as she pulled the covers over her head and disappeared.

Derek felt her tongue move slowly down his torso and then make a circle around his navel. Her soft kisses worked their way down, making his skin break out into gooseflesh. Derek moaned with pleasure as he cupped her head in his hands. He didn't want her to stop exploring him, and he wanted so much to return the favor, but he had another plan already in motion.

"I thought we had a deal?" he groaned.

"No wedding…no honeymoon," Siobhan said from under the blanket.

Derek's eyes rolled in his head and he struggled to concentrate, "Von…baby…I think you're gonna really like what I've got planned."

Siobhan stopped and crawled out from under the covers.

"Why don't you just tell me?" she grinned.

He pursed his lips teasingly, "Because, like all surprises, it's better if I show you…c'mon, get dressed."

"Reek," she begged.

"Huh uh," Derek shook his head, as he slid out of the bed and into a pair of shorts and a shirt.

She uncovered herself, exposing her nude body, "Tell me now and I'll make it worth your while."

Her curves spoke to him in ways that only they could and the temptation to take her up on the offer was overwhelming. He could already smell the sweet scent of her skin in his nose. It took all Derek's will to fight the urge to accept. He laughed to himself and ran his hands through his hair before falling to his knees at the side of the bed to kiss her hips and caress her thighs.

"Mmmmmm," she purred.

Derek stopped and she felt him pulling his body along hers.

"As much as I want you in this bed...*right* now, I promise... you'll like what I have so much more," his voice deep and breathy in her ear.

She turned to look him in the eye, "You're a tease."

"Says the woman who looks like *that* in our bed," he guffawed.

Siobhan relented. She dressed in record time and was bounding down the stairs, wrapping her hair in a ponytail before Derek had a chance to pour coffee. She knew whatever the scheme was, he would keep it as close to the chest as possible. She just had to play his game.

As they opened the door to the kitchen, Siobhan noticed Zeus was nowhere to be found. As a matter of fact, they were completely alone in the house. As she followed Derek into the empty living room, she looked around, frowning.

"What's wrong?" he asked, an impish grin forming in the corner of his mouth.

She eyed him, "Where is everyone? And where is Zeus?"

"Close your eyes," he requested.

"What?" she smiled suspiciously.

"Please," he urged again.

She complied and for good measure, placed her hand over her eyes.

"Okay...now what?" she chuckled.

"Take my hand," he instructed, putting her free hand into his own.

Leading her back through the kitchen, down a short hallway, he walked her by the laundry room at the rear of the house. She heard the door to the back porch open and the familiar sound of Zeus' bark as Derek guided her down the two small steps. A few more feet and she heard the door to the outside open. She could hear things being moved and people talking. It was then she felt another presence next to her; someone large and familiar.

"Open your eyes," Derek said softly.

As Siobhan removed her hand from her face, she saw they were standing inside their private fenced backyard. But instead of the open expanse of grass and trees she was used to, she found around thirty white, folding chairs had been placed in exact rows on two sides creating a lush aisle of bright green lawn. At the end of the aisle stood an arch of twisted vines that dripped with white and pale blue flowers. She could see small garden lights hanging from every branch of every tree and lining the tops of the fencing.

"What's this?" she asked incredulously. She looked around the yard to see Alder, Jaudon, Tara, and Theo putting various touches on the landscape they created.

Derek pointed to Casius, "A little bird mentioned I might want to reconsider our wedding plans...I thought it was an excellent idea...so, we came up with this...what do you think?"

Siobhan looked around taking in the scene, "Oh Derek! It's... perfect. Wait...do you mean...?"

"Will you marry me...today?" Derek asked, holding her hands as he placed her glittering pale blue ring back on her finger.

"Yes!" she exclaimed and a broad smile covered her face as he kissed her.

45

The diminishing Oregon sun created a magnificent orange glow in the sky as it settled in for its nightly slumber. Siobhan, who spent the afternoon doing absolutely nothing, as ordered by Derek, stood in the hallway of their Victorian home fully dressed for the ceremony that was about to take place. Derek, who had long since made his way to the front of the altar to await his bride, eagerly watched to see her emerge from the glass door of their porch.

The lights in the trees twinkled gently as the warm summer breeze tickled their limbs. Siobhan's heart warmed as she looked out into the small gathering of guests and only saw her family. She watched Luther lean into Tara's ear and say something that made her laugh openly. Abhainn shook hands with Jaudon and Alder before escorting the couple to their seats. She watched Saracin hold hands with the beautiful Brethren medic by the name of Kaia, both women looking radiant in the dappled light.

Siobhan took several deep breaths to calm her jittering nerves. She waited for a few more moments while the final guests were seated and the wedding party of two, Megan and Theo, began their walk down the aisle toward the beautiful archway. It was then that Siobhan felt Casius' gentle hand touch her arm.

"I …uhhh…I know that this wasn't part of the original ceremony," he fumbled over his words nervously. "But…I was wondering… if it's alright…would you allow me the honor of walking you down the aisle?"

His large gray eyes were wide as he waited for her response.

"This day couldn't be more perfect now," tears welled in her eyes. Casius held out his arm as the gentle music from a violin trio filled the air.

"Milady…are you ready?" he smiled at her.

Derek's heart raced as Abhainn opened the door and he watched Siobhan appear. He never thought she looked more radiant than at that moment. Her dress was simple yet expressly elegant in its design. Made of the palest blue silk, its sweetheart neckline curved along her bust and flowed gently to her waist, widening gracefully at her feet. Its thin straps glided smoothly over her shoulders just barely grazing her porcelain skin. Siobhan's auburn hair fell in large, looped curls down her back, and pinned to the crown of her head was a thin veil of delicate white lace that hung to the ground, trailing behind her. She carried a small bouquet of wildflowers with a single pink rose at its center. As Casius led his bride closer, Derek stood in awe of the moment and of her.

Siobhan looked around the yard as she and Casius slowly made their way toward the altar. Her face flushed with color as all of her closest friends stood beaming at her. Three years ago, she thought she was lucky enough to have one or two people she could trust with her life, now, it was overflowing with people who loved and cared for her. People that she would die to protect and who would die to protect her. Even Silas, who would even admit he didn't like her in the very beginning, was in attendance. She took note that he was looking quite dashing in his black suit and tie as he smiled brightly at her.

As they drew closer to the front, Siobhan raised her eyes to meet Derek's. Her heart beat wildly when she saw him and everyone else around them seemed to melt away into the background. He too, was dressed exquisitely in a navy suit, black shirt, and tie. She couldn't take her eyes off him. As the pair finally reached the altar, Casius put Siobhan's hand into Derek's.

"Take care of her, brother," he whispered, and Derek nodded.

"Everyone, please be seated," Julia instructed the observers and paused.

Looking from her son to his bride, fresh tears fell from her cheeks, "Derek...Siobhan...I am so honored that you have allowed me to be a part of this day with you. I don't want to stand on ceremony and take away from the pure happiness that we are all feeling for you right now...so, with that," she paused, "You have your vows?"

The pair nodded, turning to face each other. Out of a pocket of her pale peach-colored robes, Julia produced a white satin ribbon. In pale blue stitching, the couple's names were delicately embroidered. Julia motioned for Siobhan and Derek to hold hands as she wrapped the ribbon around their wrists and fingers, binding them together. When she finished, she nodded at Derek to begin.

"Siobhan Kathryn Miles... I had no idea that walking into that room all those years ago would lead me to meet my best friend. You have always–"

Derek stopped, his voice choking with emotion, "You have always been by my side. You have been my rock...my confidant...my salvation. I will never imagine my days lonely, as long as you are by my side. I remember the instant I fell in love with you...my only regret in life will be taking all those months to admit it to myself. I love you with every breath of life inside me and I'll love you in the world beyond."

Tears slid down Siobhan's rosy cheeks. Derek reached down with his unbound hand, gently wiping them away, and whispered, "I hate it when you cry."

Siobhan chuckled softly through her glistening eyes, "Derek Aaron Argent...I was a shell when we first met. You became my anchor to this world and showed me how to fill it with love. From the first time you held me.... that night...I knew I could live a thousand lives and your soul would be the one–"

The tears poured through her as she took a breath to steady her voice, "Your soul would be the one that would always call me home. I loved you from the beginning...I'll love you until the end."

The couple turned back to Julia, who was having a difficult time regaining her own composure as she sobbed quietly. She removed the ribbon from their hands, passing it to Megan who stood nearby. Julia turned back to the couple.

"Siobhan, do you take this man to be your lawfully wedded husband? Do you promise to love, counsel, and commit yourself to him through all days?" Julia managed through a cracking voice.

"I will," Siobhan smiled at Derek as he slid a simple band of white gold on her finger.

"Derek, do you take this woman to be your lawfully wedded wife? Do you promise to love, counsel, and commit yourself to her through all days?"

"I will," Derek smiled back at Siobhan and as the process repeated, she slipped his wedding band on his shaking finger.

Julia coughed, "Well before I burst into tears..."

Derek, Siobhan, and the audience laughed.

"I pronounce you husband and wife...please son, kiss your bride," Julia cried joyfully.

"Gladly," his handsome face smiled. He wrapped his arms around Siobhan's waist, pulled her against his body, and put his lips to hers.

The entire garden erupted in applause.

About the Author

January Kelly is a longtime writer and holds a BS in Sociology with an interest in Religious Studies. She is an avid reader of fantasy and science fiction and a lover of all genres of music. January is based in the wilds of the Missouri Midwest where she loves to embroider bad words on bookmarks, have cocktails and queso with her friends, and go on long walks with her husband, Jarritt.

www.januarykelly.com

Follow on Facebook:

https://www.facebook.com/profile.php?id=100067850730415

Instagram:

https://www.instagram.com/januarykelly.author/?next=%2F

Also By

Paranormal Romantic Suspense
The Hidden Series:
The Night They Knew- a short story from The Hidden

Hidden Intent

Smoke and Shadow

Relative Deceit

Standalone:
The Last Lament of the Late Shawn Reilly

Contemporary Fiction
All These Days